Anandam[...] and Psyc[...] California, [...] in Switzerl[...] International [...] of Geneva. It was there that she developed her love for cheese, chocolate and writing. Her parents and teachers encouraged her, and at the age of nine, her mother sold her stories to a mobile company, which turned them into audio bedtime stories for children. At school, she won several writing competitions and regularly wrote for her school's literary magazine: *Expressions*. She has also forayed into journalism by interning with *Jiji Press* and the *Times of India*. At the age of fifteen, she penned the first draft of *As it Happened in 1942* which was later picked up by Om Books International for publication.

She is currently considering adding film or theatre to her long list of subjects to study due to her fascination with different forms of storytelling. Her biggest fears include being asked where she's from, and snakes.

Simran Khanna
Green

As it Happened in 1942

Anandamayee Singh

Om Books International

First published in 2016 by

Om Books International

Corporate & Editorial Office
A-12, Sector 64, Noida 201 301
Uttar Pradesh, India
Phone: +91 120 477 4100
Email: editorial@ombooks.com
Website: www.ombooksinternational.com

Sales Office
107, Ansari Road, Darya Ganj,
New Delhi 110 002, India
Phone: +91 11 4000 9000
Fax: +91 11 2327 8091
Email: sales@ombooks.com
Website: www.ombooks.com

Text copyright © Anandamayee Singh, 2016

ALL RIGHTS RESERVED. No part of this book may be reproduced or transmitted in any form by any means, electronic or mechanical, including photocopying and recording, or by any information storage and retrieval system, except as may be expressly permitted in writing by the publisher.

ISBN: 978-93-85609-57-2

Printed in India

10 9 8 7 6 5 4 3 2 1

For my parents,
who introduced me to the world of fiction
and made me realise that every story has to have a point.

Foreword

1942 was a very confusing year all over the world. The tides of war had engulfed the world. And though, with Russia joining them, the Allied forces were soon to win, the world as they knew it was falling apart. Everywhere people held their breath and asked the question, "What next?"

In India, the Jallianwala Bagh massacre had made any kind of power sharing between the Indians and the British impossible. Both sides were running scared. Police brutality was at its worst. Congress leaders were locked up on the mere suspicion of inciting public disturbances and hotheads within the nationalist movement were urging a return to violence.

This is the time period in which Anandamayee Singh's debut novel is set. Though it is inspired by her grandfather's stories about the '40s and about having participated in the freedom struggle as a child, it is most emphatically not a story about the 'brave, non-violent Indians throwing out the bad British'. Instead, this is a story about friendship, and about how the cocoon of childhood can be brutally ruptured by politics. It is also a coming-of-age story of two young adults forced to make difficult, heart-rending choices as they take their place in an imperfect adult world.

David Wilson is a shy, bookish and somewhat pudgy English boy. He lives with his parents in Lodhi Colony. Nandini Sharma is a talkative, impulsive, fiery little girl living in crowded Chandni Chowk. Her father, a school teacher, is a member of the Indian National Congress. David's father is in the British army, but both he and his wife are open-minded and liberal, even allowing their son's ayah to take him to her home. David is introduced to Nandini in Chandni Chowk by his beloved 'ayahji' Maya who is a neighbour of the Sharma family. Impressed by David's determination to master *gilli danda,* Nandini takes him under her wing and the two of them explore the world of Chandni Chowk's bazaars together.

In its portrayal of characters, *As it Happened in 1942* is remarkably insightful. Socially insecure David tries to avoid hurting others but shies away from conflict of any kind. The fights between these two friends and the manner in which they finally make up are sensitively done.

The effortless way that Anandamayee handles the thorny issue of cultural difference is noteworthy. Both children, in this story, sense that they have something to learn from the other, and we see how they grow because of their differences.

Democracy and more particularly federalism have made modern India not just incredibly culturally diverse but also tolerant of diversity. Anandamayee's attitude to cultural difference is a reflection of this.

A book must grab a reader's attention. And Anandamayee does this through her characters, who are brave, unprejudiced and innocent. They make you believe in the possibility of a better world.

Radhika Jha, author

1

Ranchi, 2011

'*Arrey!* Where are you going? Aren't you going to spend some time with your old and weak naani?'

I sighed, and cursing under my breath, trudged to my grandma.

As usual, she was sprawled on the wooden cane chair, decked with plush cushions and a soft backing. The morning issue of the *Hindustan Times* had been carefully folded and put on top of an identical cane table in front of her. When I reached, she was slurping her tea, smiling blissfully after every few sips.

'Yes, naani?' I asked, digging my hands in my pockets.

'Why don't you spend some time with me? I may not be around for much longer, you know.'

I fought back the groan that was begging to escape and plopped myself on a chair next to her. My grandma never failed to remind me of her frail body and diminishing life span. I always found myself at the receiving end of her habitual melodramatic proclamations. Now I understood where my mother got the skills to emotionally blackmail me and my dad.

'Do you want some tea? Shanti will be here soon. She can make some for you,' she asked, smacking her lips as she gulped down the last drops of her morning chai.

'No…' I mumbled, shaking my head stiffly. She placed the cup beside her newspaper, as I twiddled my thumbs, staring at the ground in silence.

It's not that I disliked my grandma, or that I was afraid of her. I just…didn't know her. We lived in Delhi; and she lived in a small, newly developing city, far away from what I liked to call, "home". My parents had sent me to this godforsaken, regressive place for the better part of my summer holidays. They felt guilty that *they* couldn't spend time with my grandma, so they had sent me as the half-baked consolation prize.

'Do you read the papers?' my grandma asked.

'No…not really…' I mumbled, lowering my eyes to avoid her stare. It was proving to be extremely difficult to *not* squirm with her eyes on me; they were incredibly like my mother's.

'Good, you shouldn't. They print rubbish nowadays,' she said with a nod of approval.

'But…then why do you read it every day?' I asked, furrowing my brows, confused. In the seven days that I had stayed with my grandma, she had not once forgotten to read the morning newspaper.

'I only browse through the horoscopes and read the comics. They're the only sensible things.'

'Oh…' I replied, somehow not fully convinced with the argument.

'Had Pandit*ji* been alive, he would have been disappointed.'

I sighed inwardly.

It's a universally acknowledged fact that all grandmothers are the same. I'm probably being unfair. Perhaps, only the Indian grandmothers are true replicas of each other. I'd have to admit, whatever the situation be, my grandma's histrionics were making it more and more difficult to sit quietly and smile at her.

After her usual spiel about being a fragile, withering old lady, she reminisced the "good old days" and mourned at the state of the country and its youth. Comparisons between my mother and me were occasionally thrown into the mix.

'Things were much better during Nehru*ji's* time.'

I nodded, pretending to be interested.

Her obsession with the first Prime Minister of our country disturbed me. I heard her recalling Nehru*ji* at least twice a day. She complained to him about the country as if he could hear her.

'We all lived like brothers and sisters...' She droned on and on about how the world was a better place to live in sixty years ago. Funny, how she completely ignored the fact that she had more rights as a woman now than she did sixty years ago.

I counted under my breath with my head bent to avoid her gaze. It was a tactic I'd use each time; counting under my breath, quietly asking for permission to leave and scampering off before she could say no. It generally worked pretty well.

'Naani, can I go? I have to get something from the shop.' I murmured, getting up from the chair. She placed a hand on my shoulder firmly, sitting me back down.

'Where are you going? Stay here. *Accha*, I will tell you the story of how India got its Independence.' The jubilant tone in her voice indicated she had given me a bagful of chocolates and candies. Clearly, we had *very* different ideas about the concept of 'fun'.

'But, I already know the story.' I grumbled, quickly getting up from my chair so she couldn't push me down again.

'*Arrey*, things that teachers tell you these days are unreliable. Come, I'll tell you the *real* story. I experienced it first-hand.'

Sighing for what seemed like the tenth time that day, I sank into the chair for a long, boring history lesson from my persistent grandma.

2

London, 2011

The peeling white door burst open to a thunderous applause. Pursing my lips, I tiptoed inside trying not to make much noise. The comedian, who had just finished his performance, bowed and walked off the stage. I crept to the back of the room and sat down next to Georgina, my granddad's friend. She greeted me with a warm smile and quietly caught me up on all I had missed. Unfortunately, I had missed my granddad's act and there was only one more performance left.

'The next one is going to tell jokes...'

'Right, his jokes are only funny to him,' whispered my granddad.

'Granddad!' I exclaimed, turning around and jumping up to give him a big hug.

'How are you, my dear?' he asked, smiling as he retrieved himself from the hug.

'Pretty good, better now...' I said, grinning.

'Come, why don't we go to my room? We have an awful lot to catch up on,' he said, putting his arm around my shoulders.

As the man with his stock of "bad" jokes went on stage, my granddad steered me away, from the row of occupied chairs, toward the exit. I tried to open the door gently and winced when it creaked loudly. The last thing I heard on my way out was a terrible punchline.

'Where were you?' asked my granddad with a hint of irritation in his voice.

'I had to help out Charlie and his friends, they have their tournament tonight,' I answered.

My granddad lived in an old age home in South London. It was a ridiculously long distance from where I lived. It took an even more outrageous amount of time for me to get to the place from school. Despite the time and distance, I visited him without fail every Saturday.

This weekend had been special. The residents had put up a talent show for their caretakers, friends and families. As usual, my parents were far too busy to attend it, but I wouldn't have missed it for the world.

'So, what have you been up to?' I asked, plopping down on the plush, rust-coloured couch he had in his room.

'Oh! Nothing much really. The truth is we're all getting a bit sick of each other. Thankfully, the talent show was a good change. How are things with you?' he enquired, coughing as he struggled to complete his last sentence. He had smoked quite a lot when he was what I imagined to be a strapping young man. His lungs weren't in good shape. He had a husky voice, which reminded me of the Louis Armstrong records he played every Christmas. It also meant that he coughed, *a lot*.

'Apart from Charlie's basketball tournament, there's nothing very exciting happening. I got a really boring history project to do today. Some rubbish about the British Empire. It's due in a week, and I have no idea where to start,' I whined.

'Ah...the British Empire. You know, it's not quite as dull as you think. There was an intermingling of diverse cultures. Believe me, I experienced it first-hand in India,' he said, stroking his chin like a history teacher would before saying something impressive or answering an extremely bizarre question.

'Really! I didn't realise you were that old, granddad. And that you could use the phrase "intermingling of diverse cultures" in a conversation,' I teased, my eyes glinting mischievously. He guffawed, but started coughing midway.

'Well, to be fair, I left when I was sixteen, so I'm not *quite* old,' he grinned, winking at me.

'So, were you there to see all of it?' I asked, furrowing my brows. For the first time since the project had been assigned, (which, fair enough, wasn't a long time at all) I was actually beginning to develop interest in the subject.

'Well, not *all* of it. Just the last five or six years,' he said, running a hand through his remaining, frugal snow-white hair.

'So, did you have any friends? Were any of them Indian?' I asked, rubbing the back of my neck awkwardly as I uttered the last word. It was important to be extremely cautious while revisiting memories of our colonial past. We never wanted to acknowledge the atrocities we had been responsible for during the years of freedom movement, and the people from the colonised countries didn't want to be reminded of them.

I glanced at my granddad. He had suddenly lost his ability to speak. He was staring at the lime green floor with his head bent down and hands clamped together.

His furrowed brows and hunched shoulders made him look much older than he really was. There were wrinkles on his forehead; and his bright blue eyes, which danced with life and humour, had suddenly lost their vivacity.

I noticed with great worry that he had grown very thin, and looked excruciatingly fragile. It was rather strange how something that was so evident had escaped my attention for so long. It was like his laughter and jokes filled the space between his thin frame and baggy clothes.

It deeply unsettled me to see him so very vulnerable and his silence perturbed me. I don't recall having ever experienced a moment of silence with him. We were always laughing, pulling each other's leg, sharing philosophies or plainly gossiping. His quietness was unwelcoming, and the unexpected frailty he showed, scared me. I nervously bit my lip, because I realised that it could be my fault. Maybe I had forced my granddad to revisit a past he had tried to push away.

I cleared my throat and tried to bring him back to the present.

'Um...so...did you have any friends?' I mumbled, hardly expecting a response.

He threw a blank stare at me, as if he couldn't hear what I'd just said. The faraway expression was still painted on his face.

'Granddad...?' I tried again; my voice grew a little louder this time.

He blinked twice, as if trying to shake away from the clutches of his past. Then, regaining his composure, he broke into a huge grin.

'Yes, I did know someone. She was a very good friend of mine. Her name was Nandini.'

3

The Sharma Household, New Delhi, May 1942

'Just a minute!' screamed fourteen-year-old Nandini, hanging the last of the wet clothes on the flimsy excuse of a clothesline. She bounded down the stairs, taking two steps at a time. Her anklets jingled, warning the family members assembled in the small living room of her arrival.

'Nandini, get milk from the market,' barked her abnormally slim grandmother. She barely ate anything. She was opposed to, in Nandini's opinion, celebrating the little joys of life.

Like many of her age, she was unnecessarily stern and expected everyone to be at his or her best behaviour at all times. Her brows were perpetually furrowed and her expression nearly always one of being utterly displeased.

'Yes, dadiji,' mumbled Nandini, twiddling her thumbs and avoiding her grandmother's gaze.

She generally tried to avoid the lady, as Nandini usually ended up annoying her. Her grandmother was an orthodox Hindu and Nandini wasn't particularly impressed by the "miracles performed by God."

'Here, take the money. Get some jalebis for us as well,' said her father, smiling, as he pressed a one-rupee coin into her palm. She grinned widely at her father.

'Nandu! Don't forget your slippers!' her father screamed after her, but it was of no use. Nandini had already skipped out of the main door into the hot afternoon sun. The baking soil burnt her feet but she was used to it. She generally walked barefoot around her neighbourhood. She didn't want to wear her slippers out by using them too much.

She walked down to the local market and found herself engulfed by a throng of people and the cacophony all around. The bazaar was the busiest during afternoons. She was sure to stumble upon a few friends on the way.

'Hey! Nandini!' came a loud voice. She turned to identify the origin of the voice and saw a hand waving at her frantically. She smiled knowingly, and expertly waded her way through the mass of people to reach the person.

'Maya didi! How are you?' she exclaimed, wrapping her arms around the twenty-something woman's shoulders, pulling her into a hug. The woman laughed a deep, rich laugh. The kind that made you want to like her almost instantly.

'I'm quite good. How have you been? It's been ages, hasn't it?' gushed the woman, pulling out of the hug. Her maternal instinct toward Nandini was quite evident in the way she held Nandini's face and gently caressed it.

'Too long. So, tell me, how have the angrez been treating you?' asked Nandini.

'Very well. Did I tell you they have a son your age?' asked Maya, just as something tugged at the sleeve of her cotton kurti. She turned around, smiling gently, and took the fair boy's plump face in her hands.

'Are you scared, baba?' she asked. Incredibly, she did this without sounding patronising. The little English boy, barely four-feet high, slowly shook his head. His rosy, chubby cheeks wobbled, his curly brown locks bounced up and down.

'Come, I'll introduce you to someone.'

She took his soft, equally plump hand into hers and led him to Nandini. She stared openly at the little English boy in his stiff attire. He looked completely out of place in this bustling bazaar.

'Nandu. Stop looking at him like that, as if you'll eat him up any minute. Say hello!' Maya instructed Nandini in her stern voice. Sighing, Nandini took a deep breath and smiled at the boy. Surprised, the boy reciprocated the gesture with a toothy grin.

'Good. Nandu, this is David Wilson. He's the boy of the people I'm working for.'

'Namaste. Nice to meet you,' David mumbled meekly, his thick English accent rupturing his Hindustani.

'You speak Hindustani!' remarked Nandini, impressed.

'Yes. Ayahji has taught me a lot. But I am not a very good student,' he said, smiling sweetly at his ayah, who pulled his cheeks playfully in return.

'Ayahji!' exclaimed Nandini, stifling a giggle.

'Yes, my mother told me to respect those older to me.' David explained, matter-of-factly.

Nandini stopped giggling, bewildered.

'*Arrey*, stop being so mean. It is his first time at a bazaar, the poor boy is probably uncomfortable already,' scolded Maya, folding her arms across her chest. Nandini pouted, feigning chagrin, causing Maya to burst into giggles.

'Okay, drama queen. I won't scold you.'

'Good. Okay, I have to go now. Dadiji wanted me to get milk and some spices, and if I keep standing here talking to you, I'm going to get an earful when I return home.'

'Okay. See you. I'll drop by soon,' said Maya, giving Nandini a quick hug.

'Bye. Hope to see you sometime again,' Nandini waved at David.

'Bye,' David responded, smiling, as Nandini disappeared into the crowd.

4

Wilson Household, New Delhi, May 1942

Maya pushed open the heavy glass door and walked toward a wooden table—engraved with an intricate jungle scene—to put the shopping bags down.

'Did you have fun, baba?' enquired Maya, rummaging through the bags.

'*Haan*. Yes, a lot!' exclaimed David in Hindustani. He had a habit of speaking only Hindustani with Maya. She was perfectly able and willing to speak English, but the little boy insisted that she interact with him in her native language. David always expressed a strong desire to master the language. His mother didn't complain either. She was happy about her son's language skills and preferred to have him around when conversing with Indians. His father was quite impressed as well, although he himself never hesitated to take pride in his own prowess in speaking Hindustani. The locals, unsurprisingly, thought otherwise.

'Where shall we put this?' asked Maya, holding up a little wooden figurine of a smiling elephant atop which sat a small boy wearing an adventurer's hat. David's fondness for *The Jungle Book* had made him claim that the elephant looked exactly like the picture on the book cover.

'Well...' David bit his lip, tapping his finger on his pudgy nose, a habit he had inherited from his mother.

'How about the windowsill in my room?'

His eyes lit up as Maya nodded and the two went inside his room.

His room was bright and colourful. Sunlight filtered in from all sides of the room and the scenery outside the big windows warmed David's heart every time he sat on the ledge. David had a garden with a little veranda. His four-poster bed was plush and comfortable, and guarded by mosquito nets. Next to the bed was a foldable wooden table where David studied (he was home-schooled). A massive wardrobe with double doors held all his clothes. One of the doors had a full-length mirror fixed to it. Right below this was a trunk where Maya had carefully arranged and kept David's books, and souvenirs from all his outings.

David walked over to the window and standing on his tiptoes, he gently placed the statuette on the windowsill.

'Baba, we must get you ready. Your parents are hosting a party tonight.'

Groaning, David stomped his feet and glanced at Maya with pleading eyes. Maya grinned, and ruffling his dark curls, got up to extract his party clothes from the pile of toys and books he had scattered in the room that morning.

~

David stared at his reflection in the mirror, frowning, unhappy with what he saw in it. His English ensemble left little room for him to breathe. He felt suffocated like he did at the bazaar that morning. The only difference was this outfit had more lace and ruffles than what he'd worn earlier that day, so it was even worse.

'Can't I wear jodhpurs and a kurta?' he whined, flailing his arms like a spoilt child. He knew his little tantrum would not work well with his ayah. He was simply desperate to postpone meeting and greeting the guests assembled at the dining hall. They all pulled his cheeks and called him "a lovely young boy," something he truly detested.

If he had a choice, he would have opted to wear Indian clothes. They offered him respite in this humidity and he didn't look half as ridiculous in them. He had unfortunately outgrown his Indian clothes and his parents were reluctant to buy him more. He had considered asking Maya for help, but no one would give him anything without his parents' consent.

'Of course not,' replied Maya sternly, her tone indicating that further discussion on the matter was futile.

'All right...' David slumped his shoulders as Maya ran a comb through his curly mane.

'Let's see, you're ready. Now go out and greet everyone,' Maya walked over to open the door of his room while pointedly staring at him. Sighing, David dragged his feet out of his room and through the corridor, entered the enormous living room. As he stepped into the brightly lit room, his father shouted out his name.

'Come with me,' David's father said, holding his right hand out for his son to hold. David took his hand and his father weaved through the crowd, holding David's arm in one hand and a glass of wine in the other, with expertise.

'Ah, Jane, there you are! Here's David,' he pushed David toward a lady who looked as if she had spent far too much time powdering her nose. Perhaps because he had been served a lifetime of artificial smiles on handsomely made up faces, her smile seemed a tad forced to David.

'David, this is your new teacher.'

'But...what happened to Miss Mary?' asked David, looking up at his father who was busy twirling his moustache.

His father was a tall, well-built man with grey eyes and greying hair. He had a big, walrus moustache that he often twirled to keep it perfectly curled. When he laughed, the corners of his eyes crinkled, making him seem like a soft man, rather than the stern army man he liked to believe he was. He had a scar running down his neck from an injury at the Battle of Sinai in 1915. He recounted the story on almost every occasion, for anyone who cared to listen. David never did.

'She had to leave. Her mother was not very well, and she had to go take care of her.'

'Oh...well, that's a shame.'

Jane coughed, establishing that she was indeed still there and wanted to be acknowledged. David and Captain Wilson turned and smiled apologetically at the lady.

'I do apologise. David, say hello,' Captain Wilson poked David's back forcing him to stand straight. David smiled and shook hands with his soon-to-be teacher.

'Pleased to meet you, miss,' he withdrew his hand, as she smiled back at him.

'The pleasure is entirely mine, young sir,' her eyes twinkled mischievously as she uttered the last word. He was about to speak again when his mother called out his name.

'Ah, David, there you are. I've been looking for you everywhere.' She walked over to join them and smiled warmly at Jane.

'Oh, you've met Jane. Wonderful! She will be starting her lessons with you next Monday. Anyway, Maya wanted to say bye but she had to leave. She was asking whether you'd like to go with her to meet her neighbours some time. Apparently there's a girl, your age, whom you've already met I suppose.' His mother took a sip of her drink, staining the glass with her pink lipstick.

'May I go with her, please?' David put on the most polite tone he could muster, looking beseechingly into his mother's eyes. His mother burst out into high-pitched girlish giggles, pulling at his round cheek. He scrunched up his nose trying to pull away from her grasp.

'Of course, darling. You know I have no problem with you going. Is it all right if he goes, Charles?' she teasingly asked her husband who feigned to be in deep thought before answering.

'Well...I suppose it would be all right. But you *must* return before it gets dark.'

David smiled brightly, withholding the urge to jump up and down with excitement. He now had something to look forward to and help him get through the night. He was willing to let anyone pull his cheeks and pet his head. He was overjoyed.

'Isn't Maya an Indian name?' asked Jane, trying to hide her astonishment at the parents' ready consent to their child's demand.

'Oh yes, she's his ayah, she's very fond of him,' his mother informed Jane, ruffling David's hair.

'But...you'll let him mingle with them?' she asked, as if it was the most preposterous thing to do.

'Well, since we're living in India, we don't see any point in shunning its people away. The culture is beautiful and we would love David to know more about it,' Captain Wilson began his usual spiel. He almost had a speech memorised. He was asked this question a lot.

'If you have a problem with that then perhaps...'

'Oh no, I don't have a problem at all, Mrs Wilson. It is simply surprising to find a British family so ready to embrace Indian culture. Not many families I have taught are like yours,' Jane hastened to justify. Perhaps she really needed the job.

The Wilsons certainly were an unusual family. They didn't send their son away to a boarding school at the age of six, unlike most of their neighbours. They didn't shy away from India, hiding in their bungalows from the heat, the noise and the people. Maya brought with her the vibrancy of her culture, and the Wilsons did not dismiss it. They never wanted to leave India with nothing more than memories of tea parties and stiff dinners. They wanted to observe the customs, perhaps not participate, but definitely explore and experience India in all its glory. David was lucky that he lived in one of the more affluent neighbourhoods, and his father's stories impressed others, if not him. Had he been born into a family that was less well to do, with a father who was not as well positioned in the government, it is quite possible that his family would have painted an alternative version of India.

5

Sharma Household, New Delhi, 1942

The same night, in a little house in Chandni Chowk, Nandini Sharma was relishing a much less elaborate dinner with her family. As usual, all the family members had assembled in a circle and sat on the mud floor except Nandini's grandmother, who claimed her knees hurt too much to sit down. She had a special chair all to herself. Nandini called it her throne, privately of course.

Like every night, the family talked about the day's events with each other. Nandini's father joyfully recounted an interesting tale about one of his stubborn students from school.

Vikas Sharma was a teacher at Nandini's school, although he taught students older than his daughter. That morning, an exceptionally "determined" student had turned up at their residence with a query for Vikas about an impending examination.

It had taken Vikas the better part of his morning to convince the pressurised, half-delirious boy that there was no exam of any kind scheduled and that he had no reason to unnecessarily fret.

'He just wouldn't listen to me! He kept saying that his friends had informed him about tomorrow's exam and he'd come to clarify a few last-minute doubts,' exclaimed the teacher, commonly addressed as masterji by his students and occasionally (teasingly) by his daughter.

'So, how did you get him to leave? When I came back, he was gone, isn't it?' Nandini asked, tearing a piece of her chapatti and dipping it in some sort of curry.

'I ended up screaming at him and he ran away, terrified. For all you know, the poor boy could still be hunched over his books, burning the midnight oil,' masterji shook his head sympathetically as Nandini broke into a grin, clearly amused by the student's hysteria.

'But masterji, you should not have scolded him. The poor boy had an innocent query. Are you absolutely sure you haven't set an exam for tomorrow?' Nandini teased with a mischievous twinkle in her eyes.

'Hey! Keep quiet, you insolent child!' Nandini's father feigned smacking her as she beamed cheekily at him.

'So, will you be as harsh with us when you start teaching us, masterji?'

'It depends. If the angrez are still here, we might not even have a school...' he mumbled, pausing before putting another piece of chapatti in his mouth.

'What?' enquired Nandini, with a frown.

'No...Nothing...'

'Babuji, what is it?' she asked with a sense of urgency in her voice. She prodded because she knew something was wrong and that her father was trying to hide it from her.

'Nothing, Nandu. Don't worry; the angrez will hopefully be out of this country by the end of this year.' All of a sudden, the remains of the potato curry, which he had massacred, were all that he could look at.

'But babu*ji*...'

'*Arrey*, why are you troubling your poor father? Girls should not talk so much. He told you it's nothing, then why pester him?' her grandmother piped up with unwanted advice.

Nandini sighed loudly, tremendously annoyed at her grandmother. She had to interfere in *everything*! It seemed that she could never be pleased with what Nandini did.

At times Nandini wondered whether they were actually biologically related. She often toyed with the idea that her parents had found this starving old lady on the streets and taken her in out of pity. At times like these, she enjoyed validating her preposterous conjecture.

Irrespective of her sentiments toward her grandmother, Nandini would obediently keep quiet when asked to. She didn't want her adverse reactions, to her grandmother's rants, to disturb the decorum in the household.

'So, you met Maya today. How is she?' Nandini's mother, Shantala asked trying to break the awkward silence that had settled in the room sneakily, like the morning mist.

'Oh yes, she's doing great!'

Nandini immediately brightened up at Maya's mention. She was like a sister to Nandini whose own sibling had been married away when Nandini was only two. Maya had befriended Nandini a little after her sister left. They had been inseparable ever since.

'She brought the boy she takes care of and believe it or not, he calls didi, ayah*ji*!' she exclaimed, bursting into giggles.

'He does *what*?' exclaimed Vikas, whose gesture mirrored his daughter's astonishment.

'Ayah*ji!*' Nandini burst into another round of her trademark, incredibly loud and infectious giggles.

'These angrez and their antics.'

'Well...he seems quite nice otherwise. He is really attached to didi....at least it looked like that.'

'These angrez are never *nice*. They only know how to play mind games and trick you into doing what they want you to do. Of course children might not be as conniving but they could very well grow up to be like their parents,' Vikas insisted as if it was a proven fact.

'But Maya didi says that the family she's living with is really nice. They give her holidays whenever she wants and even make an attempt to learn Hindustani from her. She doesn't even have to live with them.'

'There must be a reason behind that. Who knows, they might blackmail her later. You can't trust them.'

'But babu*ji*, is it possible that all British people are like that? They're *people*, just like us. And, haven't you always told me that there are good and bad people everywhere?'

'Yes, but they're British.'

'But haven't you always said that everyone is not the same? Then how can all British people be alike?'

There was silence, as Nandini's father struggled to form the perfect ball of rice with his three forefingers and thumb. His gaze was fixed on the silver plate, and Nandini assumed he was making an effort to forge a reply. She wondered if she would get a convincing answer.

'Nandu, if there's anything I've learned in life; it's that the angrez are evil and corrupt. Their aim is to tarnish our culture and enslave us till death beckons us.' Her father spoke with an authority in his voice leaving no scope for further rebuttals.

Nandini pondered on her father's arguments. Was there a trace of truth in her father's words? Could all British people be the same? If that were so, then why were Maya's employers so kind to her? Did they really have an ulterior motive? What could it be?

A million and one questions were whirring in her mind but she knew she wouldn't get any answers anytime soon. The only person in her house who seemed to have the answers to life's questions was inexplicably upset with her. She tried to throw a meek smile in her father's direction, but he didn't even look at her before walking quietly to his room.

6

New Delhi, June 1942

It was a long time before Nandini recounted the conversation she once had with her father. The weeks flew by as school, work at home and her friends assumed priority. She prepared and worked hard for her upcoming examinations. To her relief, she passed with flying colours. Her proud father distributed her favourite sweets among the children in the neighbourhood.

Summer vacation brought with it some welcome distractions. She went frolicking around the neighbourhood with her gang of friends and treated herself to copious amounts of lemonade to fight the scorching heat, much to her grandmother's chagrin. Her beloved grandmother had given her strict instructions to stay indoors, afraid of her turning as dark as the bottom of her mother's stove.

'What would people think and say? You're reaching a marriageable age now and if you turn black, no one will marry you.'

Of course Nandini didn't pay heed to any of this. She would generally listen to her grandmother's reprimands without retorting and quietly slip away at the slightest opportunity. Her mother—her sweet, incredible mother—would cover for her the rest of the time. She wasn't too keen on getting Nandini married yet. All of that could come later, when she was done with school.

On one such blistering afternoon, Nandini was playing *gilli danda,* and practically obliterating her opponents. Her idle mind wandered to her conversation with her father about the British and their ways of manipulating Indians.

She was so engrossed in her thoughts that she couldn't hear Maya's voice calling out her name.

'Nandu! NANDUU!' Maya eventually ended up screaming. Startled, Nandini turned and upon discovering Maya broke into a smile.

'Didi!' she exclaimed, abandoning the game she hadn't had much interest in anyway. She ran up to her self-appointed sister and embraced her warmly. Maya let go of David's grip to return Nandini's hug.

'Do you remember David?' Maya asked, as Nandini withdrew from the hug. She looked over at the tubby boy and smiled.

'Of course. How are you?'

'Good,' he managed to whisper.

For some peculiar reason, David always felt intimidated by Nandini. Regardless of her petite and harmless appearance, David was quite petrified of her loud and vivacious demeanour.

Being the only British child of his age in his neighbourhood, his social skills with his peers were rather limited. He barely ever talked to anyone besides Maya and his parents who were all calm and composed adults. So Nandini, who was a completely new *type* of person, was terrifying.

'Nandu, can you do me a favour?'

'Yes, sure didi, what is it?'

'I have to take Ma to the doctor, so can you just keep David with you? I can't take him to the doctor's and he'll surely get lost here if he's left to his own devices.'

David's jaw dropped as he threw a blank stare at his ayah, a horrified expression pasted on his face. When Maya had said that they were to spend the day together, he had *not* expected to be on the receiving end of a dangerous proposition.

'Sure didi...' replied Nandini, as she imagined how awkward it was going to get with this roly-poly, seemingly mute boy.

'Great! Thanks Nandu! Golgappas from Ram bhaiya's shop tomorrow, I promise!'

Nandini grinned at Maya who gave her a quick hug and kissed David on the cheek. He attempted to flash a smile, but found it hard to wipe the stress from his face. Maya, however, took no note of it, and ruffling his hair, left.

'So...' said Nandini, drawing a line on the sandy street with her toe.

'Quite hot, isn't it?' David asked, nervously tugging at his collar.

Nandini had wanted to refute him and say it was not the weather but his multiple layers of English clothing that kept him excessively warm.

'Yes, quite warm,' Nandini opted to go with a more polite answer. He looked scared already and she didn't want to add to his agony.

He coughed, staring at the line that Nandini had drawn with her toe as if it were a work of art. Nandini tried to wrack her brain for a different conversation-starter but failed. After all, what could she have in common with a rich English boy who was apparently only interested in lines drawn on sandy streets?

'So...you speak Hindustani...' Nandini remarked, realising that she had already broached the subject during their last meeting.

'Yes, my parents are interested in your culture, and so am I. We try to experience as much of it as we can.' He spoke without making any eye contact with Nandini. He preferred staring at the line drawn on the street, instead. Nandini frowned. The way David had said "your culture" made Nandini's skin crawl. Maybe her father was right about the British.

'Oh...so that's why you were at the bazaar the other day...' she muttered, more to herself than him as there was a slim chance of a reply.

'*Arrey* Nandu, come,' one of Nandini's friends called after her.

'Uh...would you like to come play *gilli danda* with us?' Nandini asked reluctantly. Just because he was pompous didn't mean she didn't have the responsibility to take care of him. She'd promised Maya. She swayed from side to side, her hands clasped together; as she waited to hear the inevitable *'no thank you'* from him.

'What's *gilli danda*?' David asked, as she fought to avoid gawking at him.

'It's a game...like your cricket.'

'Oh...well...I don't see why not...' he said, with a hint of arrogance in his voice.

Nandini eyed David, sizing him up. He finally decided to shift his gaze to her. Nandini was certain that he would fail miserably at the game, dressed the way he was. After his insufferable haughtiness though, she couldn't wait to see him fail.

'Okay, come. I'll explain the rules to you.'

He nodded and the two walked over to her friends, who all stared rather pointedly at the English boy accompanying Nandini.

'Who's the *fira*...'

'He's the boy that Maya didi takes care of. This is his first time in our neighbourhood, so we have to take good care of him. He's our guest, understood?' The children slowly nodded, confused. Although Nandini had never said anything *against* the British, they had presumed that she was much like her father: *anti-English*.

'So, this is the *gilli*,' Nandini pointed to the wooden, oval-shaped ball with sharp corners that was placed in a little hole dug into the sand. David realised that it was very similar to the rugby ball.

'And you hit it with the danda...like this,' she knocked the stick against the ball causing it to slide across as the red sand rose up in the air.

'And then, you walk up to it and hit it like this.'

She walked up to the *gilli* and tapped hard at one end of it with her stick. It flew into the air, and upon reaching her shoulder level, she hit it again with much expertise. Nandini's gestures were deliberately slow and exaggerated. Since David had made it clear that he was better than her, she was determined to make him feel like a dunce.

David was completely oblivious to Nandini's simmering anger, like slow-cooked dal. He gaped, impressed, as the gilli flew across the street, soaring over the peepul tree planted on the other side. He clapped jubilantly when it fell far away from where the children stood.

'If you drop the *gilli* three times, you'll be declared out of the game. If someone catches your *gilli*, then you lose. Understood?' she asked, swinging the stick behind her.

David nodded slowly. He would normally have shied away from a game that required hand-eye coordination, but there was something about the way the other children were gazing at him as if he were an injured puppy, that irked him. It fuelled him to try and prove to them that he was just as good as them.

'So, you want to go first?'

He nodded, and Nandini handed him the stick, pursing her lips, trying to fight back a smirk. He ran to pick up the *gilli* and sped back to the group of children, who were now standing near the hole they had dug into the sand. He placed the *gilli* in the hole, and taking a deep breath, avoiding everyone's searing gaze, knocked his stick against it.

It slid smoothly across the floor and he allowed himself a small smile. He walked over to the *gilli* and tapped one end of it. It flew up right in front of him and he sighed with relief. Despite how easy Nandini had made it look, he expected the *gilli* to smack him in the face, or worse, smack someone else in the face.

He waited for the right moment to hit the *gilli*, mimicking what Nandini had done previously. Nandini allowed herself to feel smug now, as she knew David had waited too long. He missed the target, and the *gilli* fell on the ground with a deafening *thwack*, a part of its end instantly chipping off.

Nandini and her friends sniggered indiscreetly as David looked disbelievingly at the *gilli*. They had obviously not expected him to strike like an expert in his first attempt, but they hadn't expected him to believe he could either.

'Well...you have two more tries left,' Nandini said, breaking the awkward silence that was slowly settling in.

David nodded and, wiping the beads of perspiration off his forehead, picked up the *gilli* again. The children watched as he walked over and bent down to place the *gilli* in the hole.

He wiped his sweaty hands on his sophisticated clothes before knocking the *gilli*. He ran to the *gilli*, his clothes sticking to him, drenched in sweat. He tipped one end of the *gilli* and, squatting, swung the stick.

This time, he swung too early, and once again, the *gilli* fell down with a similar, resounding *thwack* as it had earlier.

Nandini held up her hand to silence the stirring crowd and turned to David with a condescending smile. Served him right.

'You have one more try...'

He nodded, picking up the *gilli* to repeat the process one last time. As he tipped the *gilli* up in the air, he swung at the air multiple times; certain this tactic would compensate for his embarrassment. Nandini noticed how his hair was sticking to his forehead, and how his eyes were lit up with manic energy. With a start, she realised he was absolutely desperate to win, to prove himself to her and the others. He wasn't arrogant, he was just awkward and out of place. David's shoulders stooped as he missed and the *gilli* hit the ground with a meek *thump*. By now, even the *gilli* was tired of his incessant attempts.

Children can be very cruel at times, but they can also be uncommonly nice. As David failed for the third time, he couldn't decide whether his peers were being uncommonly kind or extremely cruel. How was one to deduce people's sentiments through complete silence? Perhaps, if they had cheered him on, or jeered, he would have known what they thought of him. Utter silence, however, was not something that gave a lot away.

The smart thing in a situation like this would have been to quietly hand the stick back to Nandini.

He decided to do the unintelligent thing and picked up the *gilli* again.

'Hey! He's had three tries!' exclaimed one of the children indignantly.

'He can take my turn,' Nandini said, throwing another smile at David. This time, it was meant to be encouraging.

She stood still, silently watching David, biting the inside of her cheek to curb her guilt. David tried again, and again and again. The other children watched him fail each time and started to get restless. They began whispering among themselves, as he slowly took up all their turns. They wouldn't dare say anything when Nandini so obviously supported him.

'He should just give up. Does he expect himself to play properly in those English clothes?'

The whispers were loud enough for him to hear. Despite the hostile behaviour, David kept trying and failing until Nandini decided to intervene. Guilty or not, she couldn't let him play forever,

'You can try later,' she said, as he handed her the stick. His eyes lit up and he nodded. He evaded the other children's whispers and stares as he walked to the side, trying to find a corner to bury himself in.

7

London, 2011

'Yes mum, I'll be home by seven. I promise.' I rolled my eyes at my granddad who smiled back at me. As usual, at six-thirty, mum called up to ask where I was. As usual, it was incredibly annoying. I quickly said goodbye and dropped the call before she could say anything else.

'Why did you keep playing, if you were so terrible at it?' I asked my granddad.

I'd found this story, with his friend Nandini, quite adorable. I could imagine a rotund little version of my granddad waddling around in his old-fashioned clothes, making an effort to master the sport. He made himself sound like a poncey Victorian prince, which was absolutely hilarious. Why he continued making a fool of himself, however, was beyond me.

'Because that's how I knew I'd become friends with her and all the other children in the neighbourhood.'

'By losing miserably at their version of baseball or cricket, or whatever it was?' I raised an eyebrow sceptically at him. He chuckled, shaking his head.

'It's called *gilli danda*, and for your information she was quite impressed by my determination to get it right.'

'Failing would be a better descriptor in this case,' I pointed out cheekily. He bowed in acknowledgment.

'And failing,' he paused, an excuse of a smile appearing on his face. He gazed into the distance and I feared I had lost him to his memories, again. I coughed loudly, pointedly and sighed with relief as he resumed his storytelling.

'She was an incredible girl, extraordinarily kind, but only to those who, she thought, deserved her generosity. And she always fought for what was right, even if that meant she had to fight against the people she loved. That was what I suppose I admired about her the most.'

'What exactly…happened with her?' I asked, a little wearily. I wasn't sure if it would be particularly wise to bring up the matter one more time given his tendency to wander off in the depths of his past.

'My dear, why jump the gun? A story is narrated in a sequence, and that sequence must be respected,' he proclaimed melodramatically, which I knew he did deliberately to make me laugh.

'Right…' I faltered, trying to figure out the best possible way to stop him from getting utterly absorbed in his past. I was afraid to see him like this. I didn't want him to stop though; not because it was useful for my History project, but because it warmed my heart to see his eyes lit up when he talked about it.

'So, shall we continue?' he waggled his eyebrows at me, and I gleefully nodded. I couldn't wait to hear more stories about my adorable granddad, the picture of a pompous Victorian prince.

8

Ranchi, 2011

'Naani...I think I have to...'

'And from that day we became friends.' All my hopes of escaping the prison of historical fiction, so skilfully fashioned by my grandma, were dashed that very second.

My grandma had been telling me the story of how she became friends with this English boy called David. I knew I'd signed up for a boring academic lecture but the generous helping of personal anecdotes was somewhat of a horrific surprise.

'But...' I tried again, knowing it was futile anyway.

'Why did we become friends even after he failed each time?' She expected me to have the answer, as if I was hanging onto every word she was saying. I shrugged, as she stared expectantly at me. It was like a game to her, and I was the unwilling participant.

'Because, he kept trying and was willing to continue this exercise all day had I not stopped him,' she said, looking at me with an expression that demanded that I feign awe.

'Wow...' I complied to her demand, because I didn't want to deal with her disappointment. That was worse than any of her lectures.

'Are you wondering why I was nice to him in the first place?'

Yet again, she asked me a question that she thought I was going to ask. She had this misconception that because I had barely said a word throughout her story, I was completely fascinated by it. Perhaps, my silence misled her into believing I was a shy little kid, afraid of asking questions. In reality, I did not have a choice. Once my grandma started talking, there was no force in the world that could persuade her to stop.

'Naani, I...'

'If only you had been there to experience the excitement and patriotic fervour among people during the British Raj. You know, I participated in the Quit India Movement? My friends and...' her voice trailed off, as she looked in my direction. I immediately stopped twiddling my thumbs, raised my head and pulled my mouth into a feeble smile.

It was too late. I couldn't cloak my boredom fast enough.

'How silly of me! I've been talking for so long, and didn't realise that you haven't even had breakfast. And you've been such a good boy, sitting here and listening to me quietly.'

'Oh...no... It's fine...' I mumbled, feeling guilt's spindly fingers clutching onto me.

'Rubbish. Come, let's go inside and I'll feed you.' She tried to get up but her Parkinson-afflicted knees buckled up.

'Wait, naani, let me help you.' I rushed to her and she slapped my hand away.

'No. I'm not *that* old. Just give me two minutes.' She got up and wavering, clutched onto the arm of her chair for support. As she stood up, she smiled triumphantly at me. I bit my lip nervously staring at her quivering legs.

'Your naani can still do things all by herself.'

She demonstrated her agility by hobbling away from the chair. I was about to smile when she stumbled. I hurried to her, catching hold of her hand before she could fall. She tried to wriggle out, but I kept a firm grip.

'Such a good boy,' she turned to me, smiling.

I could have sworn I saw a flicker of sorrow and pain in her eyes, as she smiled at me. Something akin to remorse seeped into my skin, along with the scorching sun. I shook it off soon, or at least I tried to. It had most likely been nothing. I had just been sitting in the heat too long, listening to my grandma's drab stories, and my mind was probably playing tricks.

9

New Delhi, June 1942

After the *gilli danda* fiasco, David made it a point to return to Chandni Chowk nearly every day. David's parents and Maya were delighted that he had finally found companions in living, breathing *children* his age, as opposed to old, moth-eaten books. Little did they know that all he got were a few sniggers and frustrated sighs from the children at Chandni Chowk.

'You're late,' Nandini's irritated voice called out to him as he walked over to the usual group of *gilli danda* champions.

'Sorry,' he said apologetically to Nandini, who offered him a meek smile before handing the danda to him.

He took the danda from her and set his position, as the other children there spread out. He knew the process by heart now. After all, he'd been playing almost every day for the past two weeks.

He was determined to master the game by the end of summer. In merely two weeks, he had already come a long way. From being absolutely useless at the game, he could now strike the *gilli*, much to everyone's surprise, including himself. The cheers and claps had catalysed a weird obsession in him to be the best at the game.

He went through the usual drill of sliding the *gilli* across the floor, and tapping one side to make it rise. He bent his flabby knees, creating creases in his perfectly-ironed trousers.

With much alacrity, he whacked the *gilli*, watching with pride as it soared over a leafy tree on the sidewalk, until it landed with a...*thwack*. The *gilli* crashed against a pair of clay pots that were placed outside a resident's house. One of the pots and the *gilli* shattered into smithereens. The children stared at the damage done, wide-eyed and terrified.

'Please tell me, that's not...'

'Of course, it is Nandu. You know where Chatterjee aunty lives.'

'Who's Chatter...?'

'RUN!' screamed Nandini, interrupting David in the middle of his question.

The children started scampering away, flailing their arms and screaming in a manner quite similar to sirens. David frowned, confused at this sudden commotion. After all, it was just a *pot*. Whoever it belonged to could surely buy a new one.

'Didn't you hear me? I said, run!' Nandini grabbed David's arm, pulling him away with her.

'Wait...why are we running?'

'Just shut up and do as I tell you.'

'But Nandini...'

'Look, I'll explain later. Let's just...get out of here.'

David kept mum as Nandini dragged him along, racing past the houses and trees that blurred into smudges of colour. Two weeks ago, he would have been petrified and very reluctant to go. Now that he had spent time out of his house, he was willing to be more adventurous and do things he wouldn't have done otherwise. He was afraid of getting lost, but he knew Nandini wouldn't let that happen. Being amid the hustle and bustle of Chandni Chowk was helping him overcome his fears, Nandini being the biggest of them.

Somehow, her over-the-top behaviour wasn't intimidating him any longer. To his surprise, he found her *drama-queenish* behaviour quite entertaining. It was a respite from the perfectly polite quietness he had to embrace at home.

What he really appreciated about her was that she was the only one who hadn't judged him for being British. People stared at him quite unapologetically because of the clothes he wore, and the accent that snuck in when he spoke Hindustani.

She led him through a narrow lane, past a couple of shops and crossed a long street until they came to an abrupt stop.

'Where are we?'

'My house,' she replied, pushing open the main door.

They stepped in, and David gasped, amazed by the sight in front of his eyes. Nandini's house was exactly the kind of house he would have loved to live in. It was spacious, with sunlight filtering in from all directions.

The kitchen was to his right. On his left was, what he presumed, was the living room. Very comfortable chairs and a sofa were scattered in a haphazard manner, unlike the meticulous arrangement of his living room. All the furniture seemed handmade.

'Who is it?' came a voice from the kitchen.

'It's me, Ma. I brought a friend.'

She started walking over to the kitchen, gesturing to David to follow her. He was nervous, unsure whether he should introduce himself to her mother. If the people in the neighbourhood were anything to go by, she was most definitely *not* going to like him.

Then again she was *Nandini's* mother, so it couldn't hurt. He trudged after her, entering the kitchen to find Nandini's mother bent over the *chulha*, cooking some sort of vegetable concoction.

'Ma, this is David,' Nandini gestured at David, who fumbled with the sleeves of his shirt. Her mother looked up from the *chulha* and smiled brightly at him.

'Namaste,' David folded his palms together and bent down his head. He tried to be careful while enunciating his "a's", just like Maya had taught him.

'Namaste, David.' Something in her mother's tone gave David the feeling that she was about to laugh. He started tugging at his sleeves again, uncomfortable at the thought of the jokes that would later be cracked at his expense.

'Maya has told me so much about you!'

'R...really?' he asked, his hands slipping to his sides. He found it hard to believe that Maya would've ever talked about him to her neighbours, especially Nandini. Whenever Maya was with Nandini, everything else seemed to come second. David, much to his chagrin, was included in the "everything".

'Yes, of course. She loves working with your family. She says you are all extremely kind.'

David decided to keep quiet, worried that if he said anything else in Hindustani, Nandini's mother would burst out laughing.

'Where's dadi*ji*?' Nandini asked, preventing an awkward moment of silence from stretching further.

'She went somewhere with your father. They'll be home soon.' Nandini's mother went back to stirring the concoction with a steel spoon.

'We'll be just outside, Ma,' Nandini nudged David, pointing in the direction of the living room, and the two exited the kitchen.

'Your mother's really nice.'

'I know. You must be wondering what happened to me.' Nandini snorted at her own sarcastic comment.

David looked at Nandini, and opened his mouth to speak, but, ultimately refrained. Every time he said something, Nandini seemed to find a way to make fun of him. All he had wanted to do was tell Nandini that her mother had been nothing but sweet to him, and she managed to twist that into an insult.

'So, why did we run from there?' he asked, instead of saying what he really wanted to. He wasn't about to argue with Nandini. She was perpetually spouting fire.

'The person whose pot you broke is the tyrant of our neighbourhood. If you even dare to touch *anything* that belongs to her, she will set stray dogs after you. Or, complain to your parents.'

'I see...'

They sat down in what appeared to be a wooden chair decked with cushions. Nandini twiddled her thumbs, as David fiddled with an ornament on the table in front of them.

The sudden lack of conversation made them realise that they hadn't actually talked much in the past few weeks. There hadn't really been a need to talk before. David would come and they would play games. Their conversations were restricted to a few words in between the games.

'So...' Nandini said, searching for words. She didn't know much about David.

'So, do you have any siblings?' David interrupted. He had been well-trained in making small talk. It was all he did with people during parties at home. It bored him to tears, but it seemed to make his parents happy, so he usually complied.

'Yes...a sister, but she got married when I was two. I was a late child.'

'Oh really? So was I!'

'Oh, so do you have any siblings?'

'No. My parents really wanted a child, and after several years of trying got me.'

'That's nice...' Nandini trailed off. David wondered why the constantly blabbering Nandini was so silent today. It was as if she was trying to hold back the gush of words that were begging to rush out of her mouth. He was half afraid that she would explode any moment.

'Well, you're...you're becoming very good at our games...' Nandini managed a lame reply, realising only too soon that she sounded entirely stupid.

'Yes, it's rather rewarding. And I haven't properly thanked you yet, but I am extremely grateful.' David smiled at Nandini, who lifted an eyebrow at him, confused.

'For what?'

'For letting me play for so long the other day. That was very considerate of you.'

Nandini tried to stifle a laugh at David's sophisticated, "grown-up" language. Unlike her mother, her self-restraint was clearly limited. David was treated to her loud, raucous laughter. It was so unlike his mother's that he was slightly taken aback.

'What?' David asked, frowning.

'Nothing...' Nandini clasped her hand over her mouth, trying hard to stop giggling.

'What is it?' he asked, getting slightly paranoid and defensive.

'Nothing...it's just...why do you call Maya didi, ayah*ji*?'

'I respect her,' David explained.

'Yes, but you don't have to call her that as a sign of respect. It's a bit too much.'

'Don't you call your grandmother, dadi*ji*?' David asked out of genuine curiosity, without meaning to be accusatory. For Nandini however, it seemed a very obvious attack.

'Yes, but that's...that's different,' she concluded without much confidence in her voice. David instantly understood the repercussions of his innocent query and thought it best to bury the subject. Maybe she wasn't the only one who misunderstood things.

'I'm sorry, I didn't mean to...'

'No. It's all right. You're right. Maybe, it's just funny because you talk in *so* sophisticated English and Hindustani all the time. You're fourteen, but you behave like a fifty-year-old.'

David was itching to tell her that the right thing to say would have been, *'You speak such sophisticated English and Hindustani.'* The last thing he wanted was to sound like a fifty-year-old, so he did not correct her.

'Well, I apologise.' He really didn't want to, but everything he had been taught till date forced him to remain cordial.

'You don't have to apologise, that's you. And it's good, you should be different. It's another matter that I find it funny.'

David remained silent, trying to process her words. He wasn't sure if she was aware of it, but Nandini had the ability to be surprisingly profound. He was relieved that she did not peg him as a strange person. He liked how she had phrased it; *he was different*.

'Thank you. Again, that's extremely considerate of you to say.' Nandini sighed audibly at his extreme formal behaviour. Unlike him, she was used to constant teasing jokes.

'You don't have to say thank you each time. We're friends, aren't we?'

'Yes...I suppose,' said David, who hadn't really thought about it. He supposed they *were* friends, or as close as it could get.

'So, you don't have to thank me for everything I do.'

'But that's rude,' asserted David, as if what she'd said was the most preposterous thing in the world.

'Friends are like that only. They don't have to be formal with each other all the time,' replied Nandini, shrugging.

'Oh...'

David didn't have a lot of friends. His social discomfort condemned him to a lonely childhood and the few friends that he did have, were all older than him. They were the ones who taught him to say *please* and *thank you* for everything, smile and make small talk.

He realised he didn't really know much about "friendship" because he hadn't had any real friends. How could anyone consider their parents and ayah "real" friends? The idea seemed far-fetched to him.

While David was lost in thoughts, Nandini heard fumbling with the door outside.

'Babu*ji!*' Nandini got up and ran to open the door for her father. He smiled and wrapped his arms around Nandini.

'I have very good news for you, Nandu. Maybe the school won't be closed by the end of this year.'

'What does that mean?' asked Nandini, excited.

'Well, just that...' he stopped, spotting David who was watching them silently from one corner. He didn't want to intrude in their little *family* scene. Privacy was given a great deal of importance in the Wilson household. So much so, that his parents hardly ever entered David's room, claiming it was his own 'space'. Because of this, David was well versed in making himself seem invisible when it was required.

'Who are you?' Nandini's father asked sharply.

'Uh...' David was speechless for a split second, incredibly intimidated by him. He opened and closed his mouth, but no words came out.

'Babu*ji*, this is my friend David. Remember Maya didi talking about him the other day?' Nandini came to his rescue, and relieved, David closed his flapping mouth shut.

'I see...' her father returned a cold reply.

'So, what was the good news?' Nandini asked, trying to change the subject after sensing the growing tension around her.

'I think it's getting late, shouldn't you drop your friend off to Maya's house?'

'But what about...'

'His parents will be worried, Nandini. You should take him to Maya's house,' he said curtly, walking away from them.

Nandini knew pestering her father would be a futile exercise. What she couldn't understand was why he was so absurdly upset. Her father barely ever called her *Nandini*, and when he did, it was usually because he was very angry with her.

'He doesn't like me,' said David, crestfallen, as they stepped out of Nandini's house. He wasn't used to people disliking him.

'No, no, that's not true. He's just tired,' Nandini mumbled, fully aware she wasn't telling the truth.

David also knew that Nandini was lying, but didn't pick on the matter. He could see that she was deeply disturbed by her father's behaviour, and he didn't want to interfere in her family matters. After all, they had recently become friends, and he didn't want to jeopardise his first "real" friendship.

They said goodbye to each other as Nandini dropped him off at Maya's. She walked back to her house in a foul mood, trying to decipher her father's rather strange behaviour.

She remembered the last time her father had been this furious. It was the day Maya had brought David to the bazaar. Nandini had been talking about David, and her father had proclaimed, without any scope for argument, that all British people were conniving and manipulative. Nandini stopped in her tracks, as realisation slapped her in the face. Of course! Why hadn't she seen it before? There was obviously nothing that Nandini's father disliked more than the British, and David was *British*.

When Nandini reached home, her father was arguing, quite loudly with her mother. As any curious child would do, Nandini decided to eavesdrop.

'WHY DID YOU LET HIM IN?'

Nandini gulped at the unusual sight of her furious father. He was towering over her mother, his eyes wide with rage.

'Well, Maya takes care of him. So I didn't think...'

'Didn't think! HE'S BRITISH! DID YOU NOT SEE THAT?'

Nandini winced as her father screamed yet again. He barely ever raised his voice, but when he did, the whole neighbourhood could hear him.

'Maya's family. What if Nandu considers him a friend...'

'NANDINI IS A CHILD! She doesn't know what's good, and what's bad.'

'Our daughter is more intelligent than you give her credit for. She's just doing what you've taught her. She's being open and kind to other human beings.'

'I know she's intelligent. But she's just a child.' Nandini's father suddenly sounded very tired, almost defeated. It made Nandini want to run and hug him.

'Babuji?' Nandini squeaked, intervening in the conversation. Her parents turned around, and her father smiled softly at her.

'I'm sorry you had to hear that Nandu.' He bent down on his knees, holding her by the shoulders and spoke gently.

'No...it was my fault. I'm sorry; I shouldn't have brought David home.' Nandini hung her head down, ashamed.

'No Nandu, how would you know? But, he can't come to our house the next time. It wouldn't look good in front of the others.'

'Who are the others?' Nandini asked.

'Just...others. Don't bring him home again,' he got up groaning as his kneecap cracked. Under normal circumstances, Nandini would have made fun of her father for his ageing limbs. At that moment, however, the sound of his stiff limbs made Nandini well up with guilt.

'I won't. I won't even talk to him anymore...'

'Oh there's no need for that.'

'What? But weren't you just telling Ma...?'

'I'm not as crazy as you and your mother think I am. I won't stop you from making friends and enjoying life.'

'But...'

'And he might be British, but he's only a child. It is difficult to imagine a child plotting evil schemes against us.'

10

Ranchi, 2011

'I was part of the Quit India Movement. In 1942, I'd joined my father to protest against the British. It was a great day...'

'Naani...' I groaned loudly, unwilling to listen to her story the zillionth time.

I realised I had started spending more and more time with my grandma since that day—be it during breakfast, her evening walks (or as I had teasingly started calling it, her hobbles) or her daily soap opera sessions. She wanted me to be with her all the time. At first it had bothered me a lot because all I wanted to do was escape her, and the city. It annoyed me no end that she cut into my time of sitting in a corner, blasting my iPod and playing doodle jump all day long. That is, of course, until I began seriously listening to everything she was saying, instead of dismissing it as 'old people drivel'.

She dished out dirt on my mother, spilling the beans about how she would sneak out with my father at midnight. I made a mental note of all my mother's antics—dipping the thermometer in boiling tea to skip school, sneaking out at odd hours—and I knew they'd come in handy during arguments with my mother in future.

It turned out that my grandma was well versed in popular culture. We spent hours either taking potshots at Tom Cruise in *Mission Impossible* or ridiculing Salman Khan's dance moves. There were whole afternoons which were spent impersonating different politicians. I mimicked Obama's inaugural speech and my grandma floored me with her Lalu Prasad Yadav act. I don't think I've ever laughed as hard as I did then—I could barely breathe. We discussed Indian cricket at length and she recounted our victory in '89, claiming that she'd watched the historical match live. It took a while for it to get through my thick skull, but I realised that my grandma was somewhat—*cool*.

The story of India's freedom struggle was something I could not physically cope with. I got bored and couldn't care less about things my grandma was so emotionally attached to. How did it matter what people did, who died six decades ago? Independent India was sixty-four years old; the time was to move forward, not regress.

'Don't complain. Today's youth should know about our history,' she asserted.

'How does it matter what happened sixty years ago? We're independent now,' I argued.

'How does it matter? Everything you have today is because of our sacrifices! Ungrateful children! These trips you make around the world, the school you go to, and the malls you spend time in—the *freedom* you flaunt, my dear is thanks to our struggle.'

I threw my hands up in surrender, and counted till ten, waiting for her to calm down. Then, calmly and cautiously, I began making my point.

'Naani, the British would have given up India anyway, they went bankrupt after the two wars.' She raised her eyebrows at me incredulously, clearly surprised by my 'knowledge'. Sure, studying history never fascinated me, but I wasn't completely ignorant.

'Maybe, but we wouldn't have been financially independent had we not demanded our right. They would have abandoned us midway, and China or Japan would have invaded us,' she retorted.

I scowled, because I really wasn't interested in getting in a debate with my grandma. I was on holiday, and was averse to the idea of exercising my brain.

'Naani, I think I should go to the market. I need to get something. Didn't you say you wanted something as well?' I used the same tactic I had the last time, hoping, *praying* that it would work.

'Oh don't worry, if you want anything, just tell Shanti or her son Parth. They'll get it for you,' she smirked, as I slumped further in my seat.

'Okay...' I sighed, giving up.

'So...where was I?' she asked, clearly enjoying my misery.

'I don't remember,' I shrugged.

'Well, it wouldn't matter if we skipped a detail or two. The summer of '42 was quite eventful.'

I stared at the floor, her words drumming into my skull, my ears refusing to tune them out. *Perfect*. This was exactly how I wanted to spend my afternoon. Then again, my alternative choices were limited to listening to the same AC/DC album, and fail at beating my friend's high score at a stupid game.

11

New Delhi, July 1942

The summer of '42 was quite eventful for both Nandini and David. They spent much of it together, talking and playing games. By the end of the blistering summer, they were thick as thieves, practically inseparable.

'You're late *again*,' Nandini complained. It was a mercifully breezy July afternoon, and the children were enjoying it immensely after days of burning under the scorching sun.

'Sorry. Ms Jane kept asking me the most ridiculous questions ever. I didn't quite understand the purpose of it.' David rolled his eyes, annoyed.

His teacher had so far been quite irritating, interrogating him about his interaction with Indians. Her curiosity bordered on impertinence, and David was sure that she was one of those people who unjustly thought the Indians were filth. She asked him where his ayah lived, what her family did, and why he visited her neighbourhood so often. When he told her about Nandini, she grew weirdly, more interested, and started questioning him about every aspect of their relationship—how they met, how long they had known each other, whether their parents knew about their friendship, what they thought about it, and so on. It was all too much, and David could barely keep his temper in check. He would bury his head in a book, waiting for her incessant barrage of questions to stop. He couldn't stand people like her, with their false sense of superiority and no sense of respect for other human beings. It didn't help that she was an incredibly boring teacher who had managed to turn all the subjects he liked into dull, dry lessons.

'Well, everyone's left, so we can't really play any game.'

'Oh...maybe we can go to the bazaar?' David asked hopefully. He was curious to explore the bazaar. Maya had hardly shown him any of it, afraid that he might get harassed or lost in the sea of people.

'That's a great idea! Maya didi's brother is selling his figurines today. He makes them out of wood.'

'Ayah*ji* has a brother!'

'Yes, she has two, actually. For someone who spends most of the day with her, you don't know a lot about her,' Nandini teased.

David rolled his eyes at her, as she stuck out her tongue, her eyes crossed. David couldn't help but laugh. He had grown accustomed to her teasing. He had begun making fun of her too. He offered her his arm. She mock bowed, before linking their arms together and walking toward the bazaar.

'Look! It's Nandini with that *firang*!'

'At least he has stopped wearing his ridiculous angrezi clothes.'

'Why does he still come here?'

David turned around to see who was throwing these comments at them, but every time he turned, he couldn't see anyone. Nandini poked his flabby arm, diverting his attention.

'Don't pay attention to them.'

'But why are they saying this?'

He couldn't quite understand why her neighbours looked like they'd swallowed sour grapes every time they saw him. It was like his first day in the neighbourhood all over again. They didn't object to him playing with them, because Nandini would skin them alive if they dared to. But even the fear of Nandini's wrath couldn't keep the taunts at bay.

'They're just upset with the government. They don't understand that *you* aren't the government,' Nandini said, shaking her head and patting David on the shoulder, in a manner that she thought was consoling. It wasn't.

Nandini was starting to get annoyed of the constant questions as well. Several neighbours, both young and old, had asked her why she had befriended the *firang*. She couldn't quite understand why resentment had reached a new high in the past few days. Her mother had been complaining about prices going up, which her father had explained was because of the war. She thought it was a bit silly for people to complain about it. They had boycotted British goods in solidarity with the principles of Gandhiji's Khadi Movement anyway.

It didn't bother her much. She was used to people talking about her anyway. She had always been too loud, too rude, too honest. She felt bad for David—he wasn't used to the glares and snide remarks.

'But what's making them so upset?'

'I honestly don't know. My father said that people are upset with rising prices. My mother gave a lot of our rice to that awful Chatterjee aunty yesterday. She supposedly couldn't afford to get any. I think she was too lazy to go to the market herself.'

David bit his lip, feeling guilty about the big steak he'd had last night. Maybe that was why people were annoyed with him.

He could come here and drink their tea, play *gilli danda* on the streets and go back home to his cushy lifestyle. He didn't have to worry about not selling his wares at the market, or the aftermath of breaking Chatterjee aunty's precious pots.

'It's here!' Nandini said, pulling him toward a makeshift tent, breaking his train of thought. They entered the flimsy, fraying patchwork fabric tent. David was praying dearly that it would not collapse on them.

'Nikhil bhaiya!' Nandini greeted Maya's brother with a hug. He squeezed her, rubbing the top of her head with his knuckles. She pushed him away, pouting playfully.

'You haven't changed at all Nandini,' he noted with fondness.

'The world can change. But I can *never* change,' she said pompously, bringing herself to her full height. Nikhil laughed loudly, pinching her cheek.

'Who's that hiding behind you?' he asked, seeing David's arms protruding from behind Nandini's slim figure.

'Oh, this is David. You know him, right?' she asked, moving aside so Nikhil could see David properly.

'Nice to meet you,' Nikhil greeted, breaking into a smile.

'Nice to meet you too,' David took his hand, and Nikhil firmly shook it. His hand was rough and badly cut. It was quite unlike Maya's.

'Anyway bhaiya, we came here to ask you to show us some of your figurines.'

'Oh, of course. Give me a minute.'

Nikhil turned his back to them, opening some sort of a crate or box behind him. David couldn't quite tell with Nikhil obscuring his view.

'So Nandini, did you hear about the *hungama* in Burma?' he asked, rummaging through his box.

'No...what happened?'

'Apparently, the angrez only evacuated the white soldiers from their camps,' Nikhil said casually as if he were discussing what to cook for dinner.

'What happened to the Indian soldiers?' David asked, frowning. His parents hardly discussed their own lives with him, let alone politics.

'Left for the Japanese to finish.' Nikhil turned around, placing two carved wooden figurines on the table in front of him. He stared at David, who suddenly felt extremely uncomfortable under his accusatory gaze.

'I can't believe they did that!' Nandini exclaimed, enraged.

'Well, you know how the British can be. Don't you remember the Jallianwala Bagh massacre?'

'Jallianwala Bagh?' The bewildered looks David got from Nandini and Nikhil made him want to melt into a puddle and be soaked up by the ground. Thankfully, Nikhil could tell from his crimson complexion that David was embarrassed.

'It was an absolute massacre. If nothing else is evidence of the barbarity that the government is capable of, then Jallianwala Bagh was definitely proof enough. Innocent people were trapped in a park. They were forced to jump into a well; helplessness pushed them to use corpses as shields against the barrage of bullets. The only way to escape a bullet was to drown into the well. All this for holding a public meeting! If we can't talk to our own people, then what good is there in this awful system? Over 380 people died and thousands were injured. I lost my guru, my only mentor, in the massacre.'

David remained silent, trying to process the words. He could understand the relevance of the comments now—the accusatory glares, the snide remarks, the way Nandini's father reacted—all seemed justifiable. He'd naively believed it to be resentment because he was better off. He hadn't even considered the colour of his skin playing a part. It never had before.

'I...I'm sorry...' David bent his head down, pulling at his sleeves. Crumbling into a hundred pieces scattered on the ground would have been better than standing inside the tent, being the unwitting icon of those who had committed atrocities toward the likes of Nikhil and Nandini. In that moment, he didn't want to be associated with the British. He loathed the very idea. He wanted to scrub off everything that was British about him—his skin colour, his clothes, his last name.

It amazed him that this was the first time the thought had crossed his mind, especially considering that he spent most of his time with Nandini and ayah*ji*. It might be a joke, but he often did feel like he was more Indian than British. The tragedy lay in his awareness. He knew very well that he wasn't completely anything. He was neither wholly British, nor Indian. He knew he wouldn't ever be attacked like the people at the Jallianwala Bagh. He would never truly understand what it was like, being an *Indian*. He lived in a posh, stately bungalow, and had a roast every Sunday. He spoke Hindustani, but his accent poked through the holes of his façade—his flimsy attempt at being *Indian*. He was a strange, hybrid product, and no matter how hard he tried, he couldn't be anything else.

'You don't have to be sorry. It wasn't your fault.' Nikhil said kindly, smiling at him. David looked up, surprised at Nikhil's generosity. *They were all so kind!* He couldn't quite understand why. He hadn't done anything to deserve it. He returned a wobbly smile, and tried to change the topic.

'These are beautiful…' David remarked, walking up to get a closer look at the figurines Nikhil had taken out. He picked the one that had a man playing a drum. His chubby fingers ran over the polished wooden surface and its intricate cuts. He marvelled at how detailed it was. It was nearly weightless. So much so that he could twirl it around in his hands and nothing would…

It slipped out of his hands, and fell with a loud, sickening *thwack* on the floor. Flushing, he immediately bent down and flipped the figurine over to check for damage.

'Dear God…,' he murmured, picking up what was now a man with a bruised face.

'Is it bad?' Nandini asked anxiously, walking over to David.

'I'll…I'll pay for it.' David reassured Nandini, as she looked, distressed, at the figurine in his hand.

'That will solve the problem.'

'Won't it?' David asked nervously. He wasn't entirely sure, but something in Nandini's tone made him feel as if she was being sarcastic. What was the big deal? If he paid for it, wouldn't the damage be covered?

'Maybe for you…rich brat,' she muttered the last part under her breath, but it was loud enough for David to hear. He couldn't help but feel annoyed. It was bad enough that the others in the neighbourhood said awful things to him. He'd hardly expected it from Nandini.

'If I pay for the figurine, the damage will be covered, so really…'

'What about all the time that Nikhil bhaiya spent making this? Money can't pay for all the time and effort he spent.'

David was tempted to retort. The spiteful words were at the tip of his tongue, ready to be spat out, when better judgement prevailed. Swallowing his anger, he chose to remain quiet. He didn't want to fight with Nandini. She was his only friend, and he would be stupid to lose her over such a silly spat.

'Not everything can be bought with money, David. You won't understand because you're rich, and you have everything. But for people like us... little things such as these do matter.'

He nodded, pretending that he understood what she said. His mouth tasted like his decaying words—foul, rusting metal. It wasn't the first time he'd avoided conflict. He was prone to doing it. He was frightened of upsetting anyone. Maybe, he was just terrified of them leaving him.

Much to his relief, a customer walked in and started talking to Nikhil, who got busy with the client.

'We should go,' Nandini pulled at David's arm, waving at Nikhil. He returned the gesture, smiling. It seemed that she had forgiven him, and he was very glad that she did.

12

New Delhi, July 1942

David didn't think it possible, but the residents of Chandni Chowk were growing more and more resentful toward him every day. Wherever he went, whatever he did; every action of his would get scrutinised and criticised by most people in the neighbourhood. It seemed to him that the mere act of breathing the air of Chandni Chowk agitated people, treating him to several scowls and loudly whispered malice.

It still took him a great deal of restraint to not scream at the people around him; to tell them to mind their own business and to realise that he wasn't the government. He was just a boy, who sadly, looked a little different from them. The other children had stopped playing with Nandini whenever they saw him hanging around. An overwhelming sense of guilt was eating him from within—he saw every child, who had flocked around Nandini before, avoided her like plague now. Nandini always waved off his concerns, and teased him playfully for being a grumpy old worrywart. Sometimes, just sometimes, David liked to believe her, and everyone's snide remarks faded into the background. During those moments, all the rubbish he was being put through—everyone treating him like he was ridden with a terminal disease—seemed trivial. He was just relieved to have found a good friend in Nandini, who he could talk to and joke around with. With Nandini, David could fold away his anxiety—over politesse, over looking like an idiot, over taking a joke too far—into a snug little corner of his mind. He still didn't argue with her, but he felt more himself around her than anyone else.

Nandini liked him, and she didn't much care about the other children. She spent more time at home anyway, helping her mother in the kitchen upon her grandmother's insistence. Whatever spare time she did have was spent with David, Nikhil and Maya at a tea stall or the sweet shops at Chandni Chowk.

There was a particular shop that David and Nandini really liked. It had the best jalebis, and was fairly secluded, shielding David from the glares. It was a perfectly breezy afternoon. Nandini and David were at this sweet shop, eating jalebis with Maya, when the owner came up to them.

'The *firang* must go,' he spat out the word *firang*, glaring malevolently at David. He quietly placed his bowl of sweets on the wooden table in front of them.

'Why?' asked Nandini softly, putting her arms on David's shoulder, and sitting him down.

'He's a *firang*,' said the owner, as if that explained everything.

'But *he* didn't do anything.' Nandini expertly lifted an eyebrow, staring intently at the owner.

'He's a *firang*,' the owner repeated, as if Nandini hadn't heard him the first time. He uttered the words very slowly, as if Nandini was an imbecile who couldn't quite comprehend the gravity of the words he had used.

'But he didn't do anything,' Nandini repeated, mimicking his patronising tone. She folded her arms across her chest in defiance, which seeped onto her face.

'Listen, if you don't leave my shop in ten seconds, I will throw you out myself,' he threatened, folding his arms across his chest as well.

'Nandu, let's just go.' Maya pulled at Nandini's arm, getting up herself. Much like David, she preferred not creating a scene.

'We didn't do anything, so why should we leave?' Unlike David and Maya, Nandini was hardly shy of creating a fuss. At times, it seemed like she rather enjoyed it.

'Nandini, just get up and let's go,' David said this quietly, turning to look at Nandini, beseeching her.

He was more than happy to leave the shop if that guaranteed an end to his humiliation. He knew Nandini meant well, but she was impulsive and stubborn. Most of the time, he loved her that way. However, this wasn't one of those times.

Nandini sighed, and giving in to David's plea, got up from her chair. He looked like he was about to burst into tears, and that was the last thing she wanted her friend to do. Crying was possibly worse than exploding into a fit of fury.

'I'm leaving only because this *firang* told me to,' Nandini glared at the owner, who clenched his jaw, glowering at tiny Nandini.

As they exited the shop, Nandini kicked over the charpoy placed outside, sticking out her tongue at a waiter. There was a moment of confusion, reflected in the waiter's face. Then, he shouted out loud, hurling a volley of grossly inappropriate language Nandini's way—words that the fourteen-year-olds had never heard of.

'Well...that was quite unnecessary,' David said, with a tinge of annoyance in his voice.

'Why? They had no right to discriminate against you just because you're British. And you're not even a real *British*, you just look one. You're really *Indian*. The only thing that's British about you is your attire. You speak Hindustani, almost as well as I do. You can eat spicier food than I can and you play *gilli danda* as well as any other child in this neighbourhood!' Nandini fumed, evidently still upset about the incident.

'There was absolutely no need to create a scene,' David repeated himself, somewhat regaining his sense of perpetual calm.

'I wasn't creating a *scene*. I was just standing up for you, something that *you* should have been doing.' Her gaze pierced his skin. There was no doubt in David's mind that she was accusing him of being a coward—someone who ran away from conflict.

'I don't think picking a fight for no reason means standing up for someone,' the words tumbled out of his mouth before he could stop them. The sting of her accusation was still prickling his skin. Still, he didn't want to fight. He swallowed the hurtful words that he wanted to hurl at her.

He walked faster, leaving Nandini behind. He knew she was doing what she thought was right, and he should appreciate her efforts, but he was tired of her hypocrisy. Wasn't she the one who had always told him to ignore the snide remarks thrown at him daily? He was suddenly exhausted with her loudness, and her constant desire to make things better for him.

'So when someone picks on you for no reason, you choose to quietly step aside?'

David hadn't known Nandini for long, but he felt like he understood her quite well. That's why he knew that Nandini was upset. So upset that she was on the verge of a manic fury. He could tell from her voice—it became louder, and every word was enunciated to an exaggerated extent, as if it was an effort to mouth every single word. Normally, David would have stepped away, quietened down. It wasn't a normal situation though, and in that moment, he wanted to do anything but remain quiet.

'Aren't you always telling me to ignore everyone who's spiteful to me?' He threw her accusation back in her face. She blinked, and for a moment, was at a loss for words.

'Yes...but how much can you take? Don't you have *any* self-respect?'

She ran to keep pace with him, adrenaline coursing through her veins.

Nandini felt like she had a pretty good understanding of her friend. It was obvious to anyone that he hated conflict. It wasn't like he didn't get angry, but whenever he did he'd just walk off, without retaliating or protesting. He would never mention the incident again, and would pretend that it never happened. It annoyed Nandini no end. So when he seemed willing to fight with her, she couldn't help but get excited.

'It's *because* I have self-respect that I was asking you to get up and leave.'

'What?'

'We have been humiliated enough already. I didn't want to be embarrassed even further by staying there.' David was regaining his composure. He was back to being reasonable and determined to try explaining his point of view to Nandini, even if he was doubtful of her willingness to listen.

'That's not called having self-respect. It's cowardice,' she put it rather bluntly. She wasn't trying to be malicious either.

In her opinion, she was simply stating a fact. She wasn't one for diplomacy—her words weren't cleverly crafted, they were rough and honest.

'I suppose then I'm a coward,' David said, resentment edging into his speech. He had obviously taken Nandini's comment to heart.

'But you shouldn't be. You should…'

'Oh yes, because you know *exactly* how I should be. You're always overexcited, jumping up and down. You don't know how to speak to people, and half the time, you say things without even thinking about them. Do you even realise how silly and stupid you sound?' His anger flooded his senses. In an instant he lost the calm he had been trying to gather, and vomited the words that he so wished to take back immediately.

Before David could say anything else, though, Nandini's hand collided against David's chubby, rosy cheek. Her small, skinny fingers left an imprint for days. For David, that became a constant reminder of their fight.

Without sparing another word, Nandini spun on her heel and stalked away. David desperately tried to claw his way to her through a taunt. A quiet Nandini was much worse than a screaming one.

'You're just proving my point!' David shouted after her in a singsong voice, but she ignored him. He saw her figure become smaller and smaller, panic coursing through his veins. His body froze and his mind hung numb, useless.

'Do you see what I mean, ayah*ji*?' He managed to croak at Maya, hoping she would be an abettor, and justify what he did to her.

'You deserved that,' she replied, disappointment lingering in her dark brown eyes. She didn't speak the rest of the way. David rubbed his stinging cheek, unable to find a way to break the haunting silence. It was enough to make David repent his mistake. What had he done?

13

New Delhi, 1942

David and Nandini didn't talk for weeks. Much to David's annoyance, Nandini walked in the opposite direction every time she saw him. In the beginning, her aversion to him fuelled David's desire to apologise. He haunted her usual spots, and waited for hours on end to try and catch her before she could run. He had to plan things out, choosing locations strategically so as to avoid being thrown out by aggravated shopkeepers and neighbours. It got tiresome after a while though. He wasted days just trying, hoping to find his friend in the neighbourhood which hated his very shadow. His determination gave way to his bruised ego, and his desire to fix things with her was replaced by the bitterness of rejection.

He returned to his old companions—books and Maya. When asked why he didn't apologise, he sighed laboriously and walked out of the room with a book in his hand. He didn't mean to sound melodramatic, but it was a little difficult to remain placid when every second word out of Maya's mouth concerned his estranged friend. She had resolved to bring the two friends together again, but was failing miserably.

'You know Nandini was asking about you yesterday. I went over to her house for dinner,' Maya said, looking hopefully at David, who seemed completely absorbed in his book.

'Really?' David replied, turning a page of his yellowing book, perfectly indifferent.

'Yes...she says she'd like to see you again,' her tone was suspiciously casual. David knew she was lying.

'Did she?'

He flipped another page of his book with a loud *flick*.

'Yes. She told me it would be nice if you could come visit her in the neighbourhood. Maybe you two could...'

David tuned out Maya's voice by rapidly flipping the pages of his book, *flicking* louder than before.

'And it would really be great if you two could...'

Flick, flick, flick.

'Don't you think you should put it in the past and...'

Flick, flick, flick.

'Why don't you just go talk to her? I'm sure she'd...'

'Would you excuse me? I am in desperate need of fresh air,' David interrupted Maya. He had run out of pages to flick, and there was no other way of escaping her words.

'Oh...Would you like me to come with you?' Maya asked, clearly taken aback by David's brazenness. David was generally too polite to interrupt even during the most boring conversations.

'No...I think I can manage on my own. Thank you,' he said abruptly, getting up from his seat.

'All right then.'

'I'll be back soon.'

He marched out of the room, taking a deep breath, relieved, as soon as Maya's voice was out of earshot.

It was an unbearably hot day, so he knew Maya would definitely not follow him outside. The walls of his house seemed too narrow, reminding him of the monotony that would fill his life to the brink now that he had nowhere to go. He couldn't stand being inside for a second longer. With a sense of panic—which was rapidly filling his lungs—he pushed open the French doors leading to the garden outside. He drank in the musty, humid air, relishing the feeling of the sun baking his pale skin. It felt good to be outside.

The forest-like lawns outside his bungalow were a matter of great pride for David's mother. She spent hours trying to decide which flowers to plant. She laboured over the maintenance of her lychee and fig trees and the colour of the grass—a perfectly dark spring green. It all went over David's head, but he was more than happy to have the garden. It had always been his personal asylum, a sanctuary in moments of inner turmoil. The quiet and serenity of the garden helped ease his internal disquiet.

He was making his way to the fig trees—a perfect place to settle down and read, when he heard someone shouting at the gate. Curious, he walked up to the iron gates, painted a gleaming black, to find the guard shouting at a little girl. She looked like she wasn't more than four or five. She was wearing a tattered, dirty salwar kameez, and was snivelling, clearly terrified of the guard.

'What's happening here?' David asked the guard, sharply.

'David baba, nothing...this girl just doesn't know her *status*,' the guard threw a stern glare at the child, who was now on the verge of tears.

It was David's instinct to walk away, and not create a scene. After all, for all he knew, the little girl could have been a pickpocket or a beggar, and the guard was just doing his duty by keeping her away from their house. Something stopped him from moving away. Maybe he was dreadfully bored. Maybe he was still reeling from Nandini's accusations.

That doesn't mean you have self-respect. It's cowardice.

She wasn't here to see him, but he felt like he had to prove her wrong. Not for her, but for himself. *He* didn't want to be a coward, so daunted by the possibility of a conflict that he was willing to look the other way when people were being unkind.

'Why are you shouting at her?' He asked the guard, smiling at the child through the bars of the gate.

'Nothing, baba. This nasty child wanted to enter the house. She's probably been sent by her parents to steal something.'

The guard had an unhealthy habit of chewing tobacco, which had permanently stained his teeth and tainted his breath. It reminded David of the tea vendor in Chandni Chowk, who had practically pushed him out of his shop when he was waiting for Nandini. Perhaps that is why David couldn't help but feel the man was being unnecessarily spiteful.

'I just wanted to...' the little girl murmured.

'You keep quiet!'

The guard barked at the terrified little girl, who started whimpering.

David lifted the latch off the gate.

'Baba, she is just...'

'Rishiji, I think it would be best if you don't say anything else,' David said quietly, bending down on his knees to talk to the terrified little girl.

'What did you want to do?' David asked her gently, holding her shaking shoulders. Much to his relief, she didn't flinch or step back.

'I...I...just wanted to see the f...flowers...,' she stammered, wiping her nose with the back of her hand. David smiled, getting up.

'In that case, why don't you come inside?'

He took her tiny hand, barely the size of the fig he'd had in the morning, and led her inside.

Not so cowardly now, am I Nandini? He thought bitterly, suddenly sorry that his friend wasn't there to see him.

'She just wanted to see the flowers. Next time, ask why they're here before screaming at them unreasonably.'

Rishi nodded, slightly taken aback by David's hard glare. He had never been hostile toward Rishi before. David took the girl inside, letting her run around in the grass. He made a crown out of his mother's roses for her to wear on her head. He helped her pick fruits off the trees, giving them to her in a basket to take home. She clutched onto his leg, sniffling away, as he lead her to the gate.

'You are the best boy in the world,' she said in a wobbly voice, before stepping out of the gate, disappearing into the world outside. David couldn't help but chuckle, and then it struck him. This was exactly what Nandini had meant. This was what she had tried to show him, and he had pushed her away.

~

'Where's my raging lioness?'

Nandini ran into her father's arms. Laughing, he ruffled her hair, messing up her perfectly tied plait. She clutched firmly, like she never wanted to let go.

Her father had gone to Bombay for a month to help his brother with his failing cloth business.

'How was Bombay?' Shantala asked, giving him a cup of tea as he sat down. Nandini sat down on his lap, stretching her legs out on the sofa.

'Good. Bhaiya is doing much better now. I think he'll pull through.'

He lifted his cup, bringing it near Nandini's mouth and she blew at the tea.

'I heard the prices are even higher in Bombay,' Nandini quipped, as her father took a sip.

'Yes...these dratted British want to squeeze out every last paisa from us hardworking Indians,' Vikas said bitterly, as Nandini blew at his tea again.

'When will this all stop?' Nandini looked up, surprised, as she saw her mother's furrowed brows. Shantala hardly ever got upset, even if Nandini came home with her kurti torn and mud all over her face.

Then again, Nandini was aware of her mother's keen interest in politics. It was one of the many reasons that her father and mother fell in love. Shantala used to be involved in protests and rallies. Nandini had seen her father and mother discussing politics for hours on end after dinner on more than a few occasions.

Though she was not part of the Women's Congress League, (her mother-in-law denied her permission), she tried to contribute in her own way and help her husband whenever she could. This mostly meant that Shantala had to take care of things at home. What made her happiest, though, was when Vikas asked for her opinion on matters related to the Party. Nandini could still remember how her mother had stayed up the whole night to make banners for a last-minute protest, and still managed to make breakfast on time for everyone.

'Very soon...' Nandini's father replied, squeezing Shantala's hand comfortingly.

'What do you mean?' Nandini demanded.

'It means...' he paused, detaching her arms from his neck. Nandini got off his lap.

'Very soon.' His smugness made it apparent that he knew more than he was letting on. He loved teasing Nandini, constantly keeping her on her toes, burning with curiosity.

'Babuji...' Nandini whined, trying to pry it out of him.

'*Nandini...*' he imitated her tone, pinching her cheek.

'Tell me please...,' she implored, her big, beseeching eyes almost convincing him to reveal the secret information he had discussed at the meeting. *Almost*.

'You'll get to know when the right time comes,' he said in an annoyingly superior tone as if he were some sort of an oracle.

'But...'

'Just...don't be surprised when you see huge crowds holding up signs and slogans parading the streets.'

He winked at her, turning on his heel in a manner quite similar to Nandini's, and walked away.

'I missed your tea, Shantala,' he called after his wife, who tried not to laugh at the disgruntled and bewildered look on Nandini's face.

What was her father talking about? Signs and slogans? Parades? Maybe he had finally started going insane. After all, age did that to a person.

14

New Delhi, 1942

'What! A protest?' exclaimed Nandini, as Nikhil shushed her, begging her to lower her voice.

'Not just one protest, Nandu. Several. We're going to blow the angrez away. They won't know what hit them!' Nikhil exclaimed, his eyes glinting with excitement.

Nikhil was one of the most enthusiastic people around. His father had taken him for one leg of the 24-day Salt March in 1930. The passion and determination of the people gathered there had left an indelible impression on him. He jumped at every opportunity he got, treating each protest, rally and discussion as if it were his last.

'So that's what babu*ji* was talking about...,' Nandini mumbled, more to herself than anyone else.

'Vikas*ji knew?*' Nikhil asked, surprised.

'Of course he did. He's a member of the Congress League.' Nandini replied haughtily. She couldn't help but feel a sense of pride in her father's association with the largest Indian political Party. The figurehead of the Party was, without a doubt, Gandhiji, but it was big enough to accommodate several other groups, with different political affiliations and beliefs. The members held meetings, organised rallies and protests. Nandini, however, had never contemplated joining the Party.

'Hi didi,' Nandini greeted Maya, who sat down next to her popping a cashew in her mouth. Maya smiled exuberantly at Nandini, who returned the gesture, a rather watered down version of her own.

Maya had been trying to cajole Nandini, just like she had been with David, hoping the two friends would call a truce and stop brooding. She had asked her brother to help, but he turned out to be worthless. Her brother was annoyingly non-interfering and fair-minded. It proved to be a deterrent whenever Maya needed him to sort out other people's problems.

'Why do you look sad? Are you upset with your didi?'

'No didi. You end up asking me about D...'

'You girls can have your sentimental moments later. Nandu, Vikas*ji* is in the Congress League and you're telling me this *now!*' Nikhil cried out, as if Nandini had committed the gravest sin.

'You could've asked him,' Nandini shrugged nonchalantly, earning a theatrical gasp from Nikhil.

'How could you keep this from me? Don't you consider me to be your brother!'

Nandini and Maya exchanged exasperated looks, as Nikhil exclaimed dramatically. He had a habit of turning every minute of his life into a one-act play. Most of what he said was exaggerated to the point of histrionics. In the best of times, it was hilarious. At worst, it was unbelievably aggravating.

'Please don't start again, Nikhil. So what if she didn't tell you? Now that you know, what are you going to do?' Maya retorted, irritated. She had little patience for her brother's theatrics after putting up with him for, what seemed to her, far too many years.

'Di, it's a matter of principle. As a family, if we don't stand united then where will we be? Gandhi*ji* said only yesterday that...'

'So Nandu, are you going to take part in the protest?' Maya asked, unapologetically cutting into Nikhil's speech. Nikhil scoffed, folding his arms across his chest. Nandini grinned at Nikhil, before answering Maya's question.

'I don't know. I still don't understand how this is going to help.'

'Didn't you hear what Bapu said? It's about time that we stand up for ourselves and...'

'I think you should. I will. I think Gandhi*ji*'s right. It's about time we take our country in our hands,' Maya pressed, interrupting her brother, yet again.

'But you work for the Wilsons. Wouldn't *Quit India* sound a bit hypocritical considering your employers are British?'

'Just because I work for them doesn't mean I support the government. The Wilsons aren't the government. They have nothing to do with the government. Mr Wilson is an army officer who doesn't make the bureaucratic decisions for our country. He simply serves the country.'

'But the point of the protest is to kick the British out of India, isn't it?' Nandini loved arguing. It gave her a great adrenaline rush and kicked up her self-esteem, because she rarely lost. With David had gone her opportunities to argue fiercely, pointlessly. So, she pounced at every chance she got, her eyes gleaming and her words merciless.

'It's to kick the British government out. Not all British people are bad, Nandu. You know that, you're great friends with David.'

Nandini fidgeted as Maya mentioned David, yet *again*. She honestly could not understand Maya's obsession with the matter. She didn't want to say it, but she thought it wasn't any of Maya's business, and if David really wanted to fix things, then he should apologise to Nandini in person. Of course Nandini had avoided him in the beginning, but he'd given up after two weeks! *Two weeks*—that's all it took for him to give up on their friendship.

'I think I'll go. Dadi*ji* will get really upset if I reach home late again. She lectured me for an *hour* yesterday when I reached home after dark. I was only ten minutes late. She hastily got up, slinging her bag across her shoulder.

'Nandu, you should definitely join us in the protest!' Nikhil called after her.

'I'll think about it,' she bid goodbye to Nikhil and Maya, and made her way out, practically running to her house.

~

'Nandu! Did you read the news?' her father ran up to her during lunch break at school. She was halfway through her plate of puri and aloo sabzi when she looked up timidly, cocking up an eyebrow at her panting father.

'Sit down babu*ji*,' she said, giving her father space to sit. He sat down, wheezing. Silently, she handed her father a glass of water, and he gratefully took it.

'Better?' she asked, running a critical eye over her father's hunched, wheezing frame.

'Yes...did you hear?' he waved off her concern, just like he always did. The way he looked at her surprised her. There was a solemnity in his expression that she hardly ever saw. The only other time he had looked so grim was when he had to tell her that their pet cat had died.

'No...what?' She asked warily, hoping that no one in their family had met with an accident.

'They've arrested them.'

'They who?'

'The *firangs*. They've arrested all the Congress leaders.'

'What? All of them, how do you mean...' Nandini trailed off, her curiosity replaced by searing panic.

'All of them—Sardar Patel, Bapu, Neta*ji* and...Pandit*ji*,' her father replied, his gaze now wavering from hers. He raised his hand and patted her slowly, awkwardly on her back.

Her father knew that Nandini had deep admiration for Nehru, verging on an unhealthy worship of the man. She religiously read everything he wrote, listened to every speech he made and collected all his photos. He wouldn't be surprised if he came across a shrine of his in her bedroom closet one day.

'But...why?' Nandini asked, bewildered and stunned. It didn't make much sense to her. They were perfectly respectable people, and weren't causing harm to anyone.

'Because they knew. They found out about the protests.'

'What was the point of arresting all of them?' Nandini asked, still unable to find a rationale behind the arrests. Shouldn't people be allowed to protest against what they believe to be wrong? Nandini could feel the thought being squeezed out of her numb mind. She still hadn't quite got over Nehru's arrest.

'Nandu, these goras are selfish and can go to any lengths to gain something.'

'What did they gain from this?'

It wasn't just Nehru's arrest that bothered her. Why couldn't people protest and raise their voices against injustice?

Fundamentally, in her opinion, that was what the *freedom fighters* were doing. *So...why?*

'They thought without the leaders, there would be no protests.'

'What! Will there be no protest now?' Nandini asked, almost panicking.

'No...keep calm, Nandu. We'll take forward Bapu's and the other leaders' initiatives. The protests will happen throughout this month, you can be sure of that.'

'Babu*ji*, when is the next protest in Delhi?'

'In two days, why?' The all-pervasive silence was at the risk of melting in the hot sun, spreading over the muddy ground. Vikas had a feeling he knew what his daughter was going to say, but he tried to curb his enthusiasm. There had been enough disappointment in the day. He didn't think he could deal with any more.

'Because I want to take part in it.'

Vikas Sharma stared, long and hard at Nandini. She was almost tempted to pinch him. Despite his suspicions, he wasn't sure if it was a joke. She had never been as eager as the other members of his family to join politics. He had always hoped that she would, eventually join the league. He had to fight back the smile that was nudging its way onto his face. He had to be absolutely certain she was serious.

When she didn't flinch, the firm expression on her face intact, Nandini's father beamed at his daughter, happy that she was finally participating in their fight for *independence*.

'All right, you'll have to get up by six. It will take a lot of time to reach the place and organise everything.' He engulfed her in his arms, stifling her, lest she change her mind and say something that would break his heart.

15

New Delhi, 1942

Nandini struggled to sleep the night before the protest. She tossed and turned in her bed for hours. Even the thought of being too exhausted to go to the protest the next morning could not keep her restlessness at bay. Finally, at three in the morning, she got up from her bed and walked up to the balcony.

Whenever Nandini got into an argument with her grandmother, or got in a fight with her friends at school, she would come up to the roof. She'd been here quite a bit recently, trying to escape Maya, David and her grandmother's badgering about getting her married. The fresh air poured into her, freeing her of distress. She could see her whole neighbourhood from the roof. The people looked tiny. It made her problems seem so small in comparison to the vastness of the world.

That night, she sat on the rooftop, staring at the sky sprinkled with twinkling stars. She went over her mental checklist of instructions given by her father. She mused at the energy and enthusiasm both Nikhil and her father had reserved for the big day. They couldn't help but gloat at being in charge of the event. She imagined possible scenarios that could occur, and a chilling thought crossed her mind. What if she saw David at the protest? She didn't know where she was going tomorrow, but it would be just her luck to end up protesting in his neighbourhood. With the abrupt and awkward self-imposed break that they had placed on their friendship, seeing him would, quite possibly, be one of the worst possible things to happen to her. She grew tired of her thoughts crowding her mind and making her head throb. She could feel her eyelids drooping. The gentle breeze and inky sky finally lulled her to sleep.

~

'Nandini, you stand in front here. Yes, and try to keep everyone in line. No one should fall out of the line, understand?' Nikhil dictated eyeing the group of students huddled together in two rows. Nandini tried not to laugh at an overenthusiastic fourteen-year-old bobbing his head next to her.

'Good. Start marching once the people in front have begun. All right?'

The children nodded and Nikhil left with a parting salute. Trust Nikhil to treat the protest like a military operation.

'Is this your first time?' She stifled a giggle as he bobbed his head.

'Isn't it wonderful? We finally have the opportunity to serve our country! Aren't you excited? I'm so excited!' he spoke without pausing and his words tumbled out of his mouth, garbled.

'Yes it is. But...do you think this protest will work?' Nandini asked this hesitantly. She wasn't sure how people would react to her less than fervent commitment.

'Yes, of course! Don't you?'

'Well I...' Nandini was cut short by a girl wearing glasses, who pointed at the row of college students marching in front of them. She seemed to be not more than fifteen.

Quit India!
Bharat chhodho!
Bharat humara hai!

Nandini raised her placard, screaming out slogans in unison with the other voices. The energy was contagious. The sense of pride she felt fighting for her country was gratifying. For a moment, she felt like she truly was making a difference. She could now understand the zealous way in which Nikhil and her father participated in these protests.

They had come to protest at *Lodhi Colony*, the residential area for many British army officers. She had heard dreadful stories about the plight of Indian soldiers in the British army. A boy who claimed to be an Indian soldier's brother (also in the protest) confirmed how the soldiers had been left behind to be devoured by the Japanese in Malay and Burma. Their supplies had been cut off and when they tried to retreat, they were trapped. Helplessness overpowered them as they waited for long hours, counting down to their impending deaths. None of them got the opportunity to say the last goodbye to their families. Their futures were brutally obliterated because of the carelessness of the British army. Hearing the stories only fuelled Nandini's anger, and her desire, which had been sparked by the arrests, to fight against the injustice.

India is ours!
British leave India!
We will either do or die!

Nandini was getting subsumed into the protest until it dawned on her that David lived in *Lodhi Colony*. She groaned inwardly, hoping, *praying* to God that he wouldn't see her. And if she were lucky, he could have gone to someone's house, or even better, moved out of the city!

She wasn't afraid of what David would think if he happened to spot her. She knew he wouldn't care, as clearly, he didn't care about their friendship. She was more worried for Maya. She was almost certain that the Wilsons would consider Maya's decision to protest as betrayal. Maya would definitely lose her job. She was forced to push her thoughts aside, as the enthusiastic boy next to her nudged her to move faster. She mentally chastised herself. She hadn't come here to think about David. She had come to take down the British.

As they moved along the roads of Lodhi Colony, residents came out of their lavish homes either peering through their windows or scowling at them from their gardens. Nandini noted, amusedly, that no one dared to set a foot out of their front gates.

> *Angrezi sarkar haye haye!*
> *Congress zindabad!*

It amazed Nandini that they managed to keep to their perfectly organised formation. If only people could be this organised when it came to shopping at the bazaar. Her amazement quickly dissipated when one of the residents spat on the overexcited boy marching alongside Nandini. In a fit of rage, he ran up to the person's house and tried shaking the gate open. The guard at the gate pushed him away and he fell on the ground.

Nandini had been given strict instructions to steer clear of any scuffles. She didn't want to be banned from other protests, as her father was sure to do if she did get involved. It took a great deal of self control to stay rooted to the spot, but not even the thought of her father's wrath stopped her from rushing up to the gate when the guard slapped the poor boy on the face. With anger bubbling inside her, like a volcano ready to explode, she ran up to the guard, almost screaming.

'How *dare* you?'

'Get away from here, or I'll do the same with you.'

'I'm not scared of you. You want to push me? *PUSH* ME!' she banged on the gates with all her might. She had lost her grasp on coherent, rational thought. All the resentment, the unadulterated fury was flickering within her in fiery embers. It was driving her to do the complete opposite of what she was told to do. The complete opposite of what she had promised her father.

'What in the devil is going on?' For a moment, Nandini ceased screaming, as she felt dread oozing in. She knew that voice all too well, and sure enough, just as she felt her hands slip away from the gate, he walked up to her.

She muttered something to herself, as he stared, wide-eyed at her. She noticed that he had lost some weight and had grown a little taller. His unruly, uncooperative curly brown locks were, for once, intact.

'Nandini...,' he breathed, as she lowered her gaze, unable to think of anything to say.

'Rishi*ji*, why are you always picking fights with everyone? Can't you let them be?'

'Baba, I had a good reason this time. These people are rallying against you. They want all the British out of the country,' Rishi protested, hoping that *this* time David wouldn't let the girl in.

It didn't take more than a glance for Rishi to realise that the girl did not belong to an affluent family, and that, she in no way deserved to stand on the footpath outside the house, let alone be allowed to enter the premises.

'You know, someone told me that I'm not really *British*, but an *Indian* trapped in a British person's body. So, I don't think they're trying to kick us out,' his eyes twinkled mischievously as Nandini looked up, stunned. She hadn't expected him to remember. She was certain he had forgotten her. That's what he had made it look like.

'Nandini, why are you screaming at poor Rishiji? Did he insult me too?' David asked Nandini teasingly, pretending, yet again, as if nothing had happened at all.

Suddenly, the warmth Nandini had begun to feel for David dissipated. He was back to his old tricks. Back to being the stupid, chubby coward that she had said he was. She started walking away quickly, when she heard someone scream out in pain. She turned to find a man her father's age lying crumpled on the ground. His head was bleeding. Someone had clearly hit him with a stone.

'What happened?' David asked, finally managing to catch up with her.

Oh now he decides to follow me. Fool! she thought crossly, avoiding his gaze.

Someone from the group of protestors pointed to a little boy of about four or five standing inside the house right opposite the assembled crowd. He was leaning against the gate, grinning cruelly at the injured man.

'That boy threw a stone at my baba,' sobbed a six-year-old boy standing near the gate.

'All right, please go and open the gate to my house,' David urged, as he dropped to his knees next to the injured man. He cradled the man's balding head with his right hand and put his left arm under his torso. David beckoned for some help from the crowd, and two men with thick moustaches stepped forward after much reluctance.

'I'll be telling your mother about this, William,' said David, flashing a stern glare at the boy who was the culprit.

David heaved a huge breath before lifting the man from the ground with the help of the two hesitant protestors. The crowd watched the rotund British boy with his European blue eyes and dark curly mane lead an injured, wrinkling Indian man right into his house. For some odd reason, Nandini followed David into his house. She convinced herself that it was merely out of concern for the old man, and not because she still cared for the stupid boy.

'Rishi*ji*, will you please get the first-aid box?' David requested the guard.

'What is your name, sir?' David asked the man, leaning closer to examine his wound.

'Mohan...,' the man groaned, his eyes fluttering open momentarily to look at his rescuer.

The guard ran back with a first-aid box and handed it to David. He opened the box, retrieving a bottle of what Nandini guessed was antiseptic and some cotton wool.

'All right, Mohan*ji*, this will sting a little, but try to ignore it.'

David turned the bottle upside down on the piece of cotton wool. He shook off the excess antiseptic and gently started dabbing the man's bleeding forehead. Not a moan escaped the man's lips as he silently got treated. The *doctor*, however, winced each time the cotton pressed against the leathery skin of the man.

Nandini watched and couldn't help but feel bemused to see David flinch. Was he simply afraid, or worried about "treating" the man properly? Nandini wondered.

'There...all done.'

David put a bandage on the cut and closed the first aid box. The man folded his hands and bowed.

'Oh no, please don't do that,' said David, visibly embarrassed. Nandini couldn't pretend that she didn't enjoy how pink his cheeks turned—the exact shade of hibiscus.

'Mohan*ji*, there is no need. I was simply trying to help a person in need.'

'God bless you child. You're kind.'

David smiled momentarily and the moustached men helped Mohan to gather himself up.

'Thank you,' the taller of the moustached men said, lowering his eyes.

'Not at all. It was my duty to help...'

'Let's go uncle,' the other man abruptly interrupted David and walked away.

David felt a little affronted by the man's curt behaviour. He couldn't understand why he was being treated with such animosity. He hadn't expected to be thrown on people's shoulders for applying disinfectant on a man's cut, but a genuine *thank you* would have been nice. But then again, the people had been protesting *against* the British, and he was *British*.

'I'm sorry about that...' Nandini broke his train of thought.

'Huh...oh...it's fine.'

It looked like she wanted to say something else, but the words dissolved at the tip of the tongue. David could tell that she was nervous and struggling with her thoughts. He had a feeling her apology was not just about the behaviour of the moustached man, but something entirely different.

'So, it's been a long time...' she said, emulating the moustached man's manner of staring at the ground.

'Yes...and I'm up here, not down there.' David couldn't resist being a little mean; after all, she *had* made him chase her all around *Chandni Chowk* for days on end.

'I...I know...' she faltered, sighed, and looked up at him.

'We haven't talked for so long...'

'That is true,' David nodded.

Nandini was burning with discomfort while David waited for her to say something. As both of them stood silently, they could distantly hear the protestors resuming their clarion call for *freedom* in the distance.

The protestors' slogans made the situation even more awkward, the tension palpable. While Nandini decided to study the nearby flowerbed, David tried to swat away a fly. Both of them had run out of excuses to avoid each other. David desperately wanted it to go away—the feeling that Nandini was a stranger, someone who belonged to the opposite camp. He couldn't ignore the fact that they were standing inside his house, the very monument of British colonialism that she was protesting against. She was part of the people screaming on the other side of the gate, and he was trapped, caged inside the grand bungalow against his will.

Nandini was aware of his *Britishness*. No matter what she said, he lived in *Lodhi Colony*, not Chandni Chowk. He was wearing a pantsuit, not a khadi kurta. He had servants and an ayah at his disposal, and he would never be affected by Pandit*ji*'s imprisonment. He probably didn't even know who Pandit*ji* was; it wasn't a subject they had discussed. But he'd helped the old man, despite what his neighbours or the guard thought of him. He was not a *coward* after all. He'd never been anything but kind to Maya didi and her, and the least he deserved was a *thank you*.

'But what you did today was very...it was very nice...' she dropped her gaze to the ground again; she deliberately refrained from looking at David's face. She was almost certain that he would laugh viciously at her, or worse treat her like she was an alien creature, someone he didn't know.

'Well...I suppose, but he would have...'

'And it was very brave,' she interrupted without meaning to, and instantly started blushing. He couldn't help but smirk.

'Really? But I thought I'm a coward,' he feigned surprise, taking care to use the exact word she had used to describe him. He could see her fumbling uncomfortably with her fingers, but wanted to carry on with the act a little longer just for fun.

'I...I guess...' she hesitated, looking at him—her big, dark brown eyes, entreating him to not make her say it. She knew exactly what he wanted her to say, but she couldn't bring herself to do it. Her pride came in the way.

'You guess...?' David played along. He was not going to let her get away with all that she had said so easily. Not today. She had worked him hard and still not forgiven him. He wasn't going to *forgive* her before she just *said* those three words.

'Fine. I was...I was wrong,' she grumbled.

Perhaps that was not the manner in which he wanted her to apologise, but it was precisely what he'd wanted to hear.

Shrugging, he accepted her attempt at amending things. It was the best he was going to get out of her anyway.

'Ah...I see...' he tried not to make a show, stifling the grin that was begging to spill forth.

'I...I suppose I'll see you around?' she asked hopefully. David smiled and nodded, and she grinned back at him. She eyed the crowd of protestors and bit her lip uneasily.

'Nandini, go. You've made a commitment and I know it's not against me, it's against the government,' David urged Nandini, who smiled and ran after the crowd.

She sincerely hoped David meant what he said. She wasn't really *protesting* against the British. She was raising a voice against the government. She *knew* that all British people couldn't be bad, and after today's episode she was confident that at least a few other protestors would have had a change of heart toward the British. After all, how couldn't they—an English boy had helped one of their own. What she had forgotten in her glee at getting her best friend back was that another British boy had been the cause of the problem. People weren't going to remember the kindness of David but they would never forget the callousness of the other young boy.

~

'Nandini! What were you doing?' exclaimed Nikhil, grabbing Nandini by her arm and pulling her aside from the assembled crowd.

Nandini didn't know what to say. How could she justify her actions? She had momentarily ditched a group of protestors to go converse with a British boy. In her mind, she convinced herself by saying that, David wasn't truly British. He was just trapped in the body of a firang, but he had the heart of an Indian.

'I...you know... David helped that man...so I was just...'

'Nandini! This is a *protest*! You can't...,' he sighed, clenching and unclenching his fists in what Nandini knew was an attempt to calm down.

'Nandu, if your father finds out about this...' Nikhil took on a stern tone, almost identical to Nandini's father. He faltered, however, when he saw Nandini's big brown eyes, simmering in guilt.

He relented, stroking her hair. For the first time that day, Nandini noticed the dark circles under his eyes that made him look ten times his age. She hadn't grasped the gravity of the situation and how Nikhil and her father had toiled to organise this protest march. All the big leaders had been arrested, so the onus of staging such movements rested on the Congress members.

'I'm sorry, bhaiya...but I felt we should thank him.'

David had helped their comrade, and it was only good manners to thank him, thought Nandini. After all, isn't that what her father had always taught her?

'Nandu, sometimes...' he paused in an effort to find the right words.

'Sometimes, Nandini, we shouldn't do what we *feel* is right, because we...might be wrong.'

'So, what I did was wrong?' asked a puzzled Nandini, stung by what Nikhil had just said.

'No, not necessarily, but...sometimes...we have to think about the *consequences* of our actions.'

Nikhil tried to be patient and serious. Nandini frowned, still unable to follow. Perhaps, Nandini's lack of a response bothered Nikhil, so he spoke again.

'Anyway, let's go. We can't just stand here in the middle of a protest we're supposed to be a part of,' he continued, dropping the matter for the moment.

'But…' she was interrupted by Nikhil who nudged her back into the crowd. Loud chants of slogans muted her half-spoken words.

Nikhil rushed ahead, prodding and pushing people into line, trying to maintain some semblance of the organisation they had miraculously managed to maintain before the incident with the old man.

His brow seemed perpetually furrowed, as he slid in between the throng of people, and Nandini couldn't help but wonder if he was right. Did it truly matter what people thought of you? She had never been bothered by it, and had never before been told to worry. Was this just a grown up thing? Then why had her father always encouraged her to trust her judgement? She shook her thoughts away as someone prodded her to move forward. For Nandini, the surrounding political events in the wake of the on-going Independence struggle could not convince her to go against everything she believed in. Just because everything around her was changing didn't mean that she had to change too.

16

New Delhi, 1942

Nandini bit her lip nervously, as Maya squeezed her hand in an attempt to be comforting.

'Keep calm Nandu, he won't be upset, *trust* me.'

Nandini wasn't so sure whether she could trust Maya or not, largely because Maya didn't sound too certain herself. She had decided to go pay David a visit, and apologise properly. The flimsy, half apology that she had strung together on the day of the protest was, in her opinion, not good enough. He had already attempted to apologise, so it was only fair if she gave it a shot this time. The only problem was that she was scared out of her wits about how he would react. She was quite certain that he would push her out, without really listening to her apology at all.

She walked the same street of *Lodhi Colony* that she had marched through only a week ago during the protest. Nandini marvelled at how different the street looked without over a thousand people traipsing through it, shouting slogans. There was a certain quietness that had settled in the neighbourhood. a sort of eerie calm. It was very different from her Chandni Chowk, where people were clamouring everywhere, and noise was a constant presence. For a moment, she considered the possibility that everyone was actually in hiding, afraid of another protest.

'Are you sure he'll be at home?' Nandini asked Maya.

'Of course. He doesn't go out much, except to Chandni Chowk to see you or me,' Maya replied, smiling at the guard standing on the other side of the black, iron gate. Nandini struggled to remember his name, as he turned the latch of the gate, opening it for them.

'Hello Maya, quite late today, aren't you?'

'Yes, had to pick up this little one from school. She wanted to come meet David.'

As Nandini stepped inside the Wilson bungalow, she couldn't help but let out a gasp. From the outside itself, their house looked beautiful. They had a garden the size of her street. It could either be a huge park or a small forest. Birds were perched on nearly every tree, chirping enthusiastically. There were roses, marigolds, and a little pond for lotuses to grow in. She could swear that she saw footprints of an animal (suspiciously) identical to those of a fox on a muddy path near the pond. It was a wonderland, just like the one she had read about in a book. It explained why David didn't go out much. Had Nandini been in David's place, she would've stayed inside and run around the garden all day.

'Nandini, stop gawking and come inside,' Maya tugged at her hand, pulling her toward the front door of the house. Embarrassed, Nandini followed Maya, but paused in her tracks to examine the footprints closely.

'Stop it Nandu, this is not a zoo,' Maya scolded, as they reached the front door, which was surprisingly half-open.

'Aren't they afraid of thieves?' Nandini asked, taken aback to see the front door of the house open.

'That's what the guard is for,' Maya muttered, pushing through the door..

'Oh...of course...' Nandini mumbled, feeling incredibly stupid, and not for the first time, completely out of place.

'I think David is through with his lessons for the day, so why don't you come with me to his room?'

Nandini nodded, clinging onto Maya's arm. They walked through the hallway, passing briefly through the dining hall, before making their way into another hallway.

'This house is huge! How do you not get lost in it?' Nandini whispered.

'You get used to it.'

Nandini couldn't help but be a little impressed with Maya. If she were in her place, she would have been dwarfed by the immensity and opulence of the house. She would be afraid to touch anything, lest she break it.

They walked past several closed, creamy-white doors, pausing at one that was left ajar.

'I heard there was a protest here a week ago,' a woman's voice drifted out of the door, and Nandini moved closer, trying to get a good look at her.

'Yes...' came David's voice, somewhat irritated and confused at this question being thrown at him.

'And you helped one of the protestors...at least that's what I heard,' the woman added the last part hastily, like an afterthought.

'I most certainly did,' David replied coldly. Nandini could imagine his eyes slanting, his brows furrowing, and his jaw clenching in anger.

'I...see...' the woman seemed to be at a loss for words after the unexpected reply. There was silence, filled by the creaking of chairs as the two opposing occupants shifted uncomfortably in them.

'Well, if we're done with today's lessons...' David broke the silence, trying his best to articulate his desire, for her to leave, in a polite way. Clearly, he was finding it very difficult.

'Ah...yes, of course.'

Nandini heard the woman get up from her seat, the chair groaning. She heard her heels clatter against the marble floor, getting louder as she approached the door. She saw the door handle turn and stop midway.

'What you did is commendable, Mr Wilson.'

There was a pregnant pause, but Nandini could nearly *feel* David's surprise.

'Thank you,' David responded, just as Nandini had guessed. Nandini wondered why he was surprised, but before she could ask Maya, the door opened and a very beautiful lady in her early-thirties walked out.

'Ah, hello Maya.'

She smiled in a manner that made the smile seem more like a grimace. It was as if it put the woman in physical pain to smile at Maya.

'Hello, memsahib,' Maya smiled curtly at the lady, who nodded and walked away.

'Come, let's go inside.'

Nandini nodded, attempting to move, but suddenly losing all sensation in her legs.

'Ayah*ji*!' David exclaimed, smiling brightly at her, as she entered the room. Maya smiled back, pulling Nandini inside.

'Oh, hello...'

Nandini smiled meekly at David, who got up from his seat and walked toward her. She fought back a giggle at seeing what he was wearing—a tight waistcoat over a long, starched white shirt and pants. He looked quite silly.

'Nice clothes...' Nandini stifled her laughter. David pulled at the sleeves of his shirt defensively, pursing his lips.

'Hilarious. My tutor prefers that I observe rules of a proper Englishman when around her,' he explained defensively.

'Well, I'll be in the kitchen. I have to prepare your lunch.'

Smiling, Maya left the room. She felt that the two needed a little privacy in order to patch up. Silence engulfed the room the moment Maya left. Nandini, out of habit, started twiddling her thumbs. David continued pulling at his sleeves, staring furiously at the white laces on his shiny black shoes.

'So, what brings you here?' David coughed, clearing his throat, before posing the question.

Nandini bit at her lip again, uncertain about how to phrase her apology. To say that she hadn't practised saying *sorry* in front of the mirror at eleven in the night would be a blatant lie. She had indeed spent the better part of her evening trying out different ways to apologise to David.

'I thought I'd...I wanted to...to say sorry.' She mumbled the last words, all in one breath. David arched his right eyebrow, throwing an incredulous, questioning look at Nandini. Exasperated, Nandini launched into her second attempt at an apology.

'I felt it would be best if I...well, it was really Maya didi who told me I should say sorry...' Nandini trailed off, unable to add anything more to her sad, pathetic sentence.

'I'm sorry...did you just apologise to me?' David asked, genuinely confused. Knowing Nandini, an apology was something bordering on the far-fetched. Her *self-respect* and stubbornness wouldn't allow for it. Then again, hadn't she just included the word *sorry* in her not-so-eloquent discourse?

'David, I'm not going to repeat myself. I know you understood what I meant.' Nandini scowled darkly, her apologetic mood quickly transforming into a foul one.

'Well, I suppose then, that it *was* an apology,' David mused, as Nandini rolled her eyes, a small smile emerging on her lips.

'You're such a drama queen,' she playfully teased him, and he chuckled good-humouredly.

'Well, you were the one who decided to apologise. You admitting your mistake was enough of an apology for me.'

'I know...but I felt I should.'

'There was no reason for you to feel bad. In a way, you were right.'

'Did I just hear, *right*? What did you just say?' Nandini wrung her ears, leaning in closer to David. David shook his head, amused.

'I suppose, in a certain way, you were right as well,' he reluctantly replied, as Nandini's eyes lit up, a gleeful smile appearing on her face.

'In *what* way exactly?' she continued. It felt good to have her friend back. Now she could tease him mercilessly.

'You were right, I shy away from fights, and sometimes, that stops me from standing up for what's right. And...well... living.'

David's tone suddenly changed from mildly-annoyed to serious and sincere. It was amazing how quickly he could do that.

'Well, I suppose I should tell you, once again, that you are *not* a coward. When I said that, I didn't realise that bravery could be shown in different ways.' Nandini paused, gesticulating wildly with her hands. It was as if she was struggling to catch the words, and pin them down to explain her thoughts.

'What I mean is that...you don't have to shout from the rooftops in order to do something brave. When you helped that man at the protest, you weren't fighting or screaming or getting angry. You just...*acted* immediately, in the way most fit for the situation.'

Nandini looked at David, urging a clue from him on whether he understood what she was saying.

'Right...' David replied. He understood what Nandini was trying to say. He was also tired of the whole incident. He wanted to forget all about it. It was time to bury the hatchet.

~

Nandini spent quite an amicable afternoon at the Wilson's bungalow. David took her on a tour of his massive bungalow and the garden. David disproved her suspicions about the footprints in the mud, claiming that it was nearly impossible for a fox to venture into the gardens in *Lodhi Colony*. As she was leaving, David's mother returned from her afternoon tea, and was absolutely delighted to meet Nandini.

'Mother, this is my friend Nandini.' David awkwardly introduced Nandini to his mother, whose face immediately lit up, as if in recognition. It was apparent that she had been told quite a lot about Nandini.

'Ah, of course! Maya and David have told me a lot about you. It is wonderful to finally meet you!'

She enveloped Nandini into an overbearing hug, her strong perfume wafting in Nandini's nose. As she let go, Nandini smiled warmly, trying to shake the smell of her perfume off herself.

'Very nice to meet you too.'

'So, what brings you here? Isn't David usually the one who goes over to your neighbourhood? Planning another protest, are you?'

Nandini blinked, a little shaken by her question. Although she was smiling, Nandini couldn't help but wonder if the protests had bothered her. Maybe she was just being paranoid.

'Oh, I'm just joking silly. As we told Maya, the protests are not aimed at us, so we really don't have a problem.'

'Well...that's extremely kind of you. Not all people in the neighbourhood think so.'

'Yes, I am aware of what happened the other day. I'm terribly sorry. Although I heard my little David was quite the hero,' David's mother replied fondly, pinching David's relatively chubby cheek. David scowled, pulling her hand off his cheek, as Nandini laughed.

'All right, I think it's time we go,' David said, hastily, before his mother could do anything else that would be etched in his memory as absolutely mortifying.

'It was really nice to meet you Nandini. Do come again.'

As Nandini walked out of the gate with Maya, she marvelled at how different David's mother had been in comparison to her father. While her father had been hostile, David's mother was cordial and generous. She hoped that David's mother would always be so kind. It made things for Nandini, and Maya, much easier.

17

Chandni Chowk, New Delhi, September 1942

Nandini walked up to her father, handing him a white envelope folded in half. Her father pinched her left cheek causing Nandini to scowl. She started walking away, very slowly, looking over as her father tore the flap of the envelope. He looked up at her, and she immediately turned away.

'Nandini, you know the rules,' he said sternly, as she stopped in her tracks.

'But you know you can trust me babuji...' Nandini whined, facing her father and pouting in a way that she knew often worked wonders.

'We've been over this Nandu...' her father sighed, his voice strained and tired. Unlike Nandini, he didn't particularly enjoy the exchange that took place between them every time Nandini came with a letter.

'But you always used to tell me what's happening in the Party before...' Nandini complained, the expression on her face forlorn.

'Nandu...' he hoped his strict, disciplinarian tone would work on his daughter. It was really for her own safety that he was being so secretive.

Much to Vikas' relief, Nandini relented, and slouching, quietly sat on the floor by her father's feet. Little did he know that this was merely a tactic—something she had devised quite perfectly over the course of many hours. She was certain that her brilliant strategy would help her wriggle out the secrets locked within the lines of the letters she delivered to her father.

'But babu*ji*, you know I won't tell anyone. Don't you *trust* me?' Nandini beseeched, widening her large brown eyes, threatening to spill tears.

'It's not about trust Nandini,' her father fought back a smile, amused at her tactics. Like Nandini, he had a few tricks up his sleeve as well.

'Then what is it? What's so important that you can't tell me even if you trust me?' Nandini asked, now getting visibly impatient. Her excellent plan hadn't taken her impatience into account.

'It's dangerous. The British would jail you if they got hold of the information in these letters.'

'But I'm just a child; they can't throw me in jail!' Nandini tried to argue, knowing very well that her father had a rebuttal ready.

'Even then, what if it reaches the British? Our whole family would get into trouble, and I would probably be sent to jail. Would you want your father to rot in jail?'

Nandini grumbled loudly, unable to think of anything else to say or do. She felt disappointed, in herself and her father. He was so adamant about keeping secrets from her that she stooped as low as using *emotional blackmail*. It was a well-known fact between the pair that *blackmail* was a weapon used only in immeasurably desperate times. Not that it was going to stop her from doing the same thing as he was.

'But they won't find out. Babu*ji*, why don't you trust me? Am I not your daughter? Do you really think I would let you go to jail?'

Her father paused, trying to find the best way to answer her question. For once, in the argument, he was at a loss for words. He had not expected Nandini to counter, using his strategy on him.

'Of course I trust you, but...I don't trust that *firang* boy you're always with.'

He smirked, satisfied with his retort. He had touched the one topic that Nandini and he strongly debated—her friendship with Maya's employer's son. He had given her permission to be friends with him, but had made it clear on several occasions that he did not favour the friendship, especially after the little fight Nandini and David had had in the middle. Although Nandini hadn't told her father anything, he knew she was upset. He couldn't stand seeing her like that—quiet, submissive and completely unenthusiastic. He'd been quite tempted to tell her not to forgive the idiotic firang, and had almost done so, when his wife knocked some sense into him. Nandini had the right to make her own mistakes and he was not allowed to interfere.

'But I won't tell him, babu*ji*. Just because we're friends doesn't mean I tell him everything!' Nandini exclaimed, somewhat agitated. Her father raised an eyebrow at her, his expression incredulous.

'All right, we might talk about a lot of things, but I can assure you, I wouldn't tell him about something this important.' Nandini pressed on, determined to extract at least a scrap of information from her tight-lipped father *this* time.

'Nandini...' her father sighed for what appeared to be the hundredth time, his resolve wearing off. He was under strict instructions to not divulge any details to family members, but he knew his daughter wouldn't give in. He had to say something to quell her curiosity. Cupping his daughter's face in his hands, he started speaking, his tone gentler than before.

'Listen, now that the main Congress leaders have been arrested, it's up to the other members to take the ideals of the struggle forward. But we don't want to be arrested as well, because then, there won't be anyone *left* to lead the protests. So, we work in secret, and under no circumstances can we discuss what we do with anyone. Not even with incredibly intelligent, trustworthy little girls like you.'

Nandini smiled, and her father heaved a sigh of relief. He didn't remember the last time she had quietly acquiesced. It was normally a never-ending uphill battle with his daughter, especially now that she had a keen interest in his work.

'Fine, babuji. But tell me, why have you been asking *me* to bring you all the letters?'

'Because no one suspects children.'

'But, isn't there a possibility that I could read your letters? Aren't you afraid that one day I might?'

'Nandu, there's a very good reason no one suspects children. They're innocent, and if you explain something to them properly and kindly, they will listen obediently,' her father said, very pointedly. If Nandini hadn't been so agitated, she might have laughed at her father's thinly veiled attempts to get her to "behave".

'But what if I just...'

'If you opened one of my letters I would know from just seeing the envelope, and I wouldn't send you to fetch them again. As it is, you wouldn't understand anything written in these letters. They're coded.'

Nandini sighed loudly, heavily, giving up on the argument. She had tried time and again, and now she was willing to quit pestering her father. Maybe it was all for the best.

'I'll leave you alone with your letter then.'

With that, she got up and made her way to the main door.

'Don't push him right now, Nandu. He is under a lot of pressure.'

Nandini's parting withering glare at her mother reflected the resentment and frustration she felt toward her father. To her surprise, her mother just smiled at her openly impudent act.

'Thank your stars that you do more than painting posters and cooking for the Party members.'

Nandini frowned. She knew her mother did a lot more than that. She'd heard her grandmother complain about her mother's participation in the activities of the Congress Party on more than one occasion. Perhaps that had been before she was married to Nandini's father.

'You do more than that, don't you Ma?' Nandini asked, fighting to keep the concern out of her voice.

'Yes, I do. Now go play.'

At that, Nandini had no choice but to sigh and walk away. She was unimaginably frustrated with her parents treating her like a child, who couldn't form her own opinions or thoughts. Whenever her parents wanted to shoo her away, she was told to "go play". It didn't truly matter though. She had devised other strategies to obtain the information she required. So what if her father was unwilling to spill the beans? She had another reliable source, who she was convinced would not be a hard nut to crack.

~

'Nikhil bhaiya!' Nandini shouted in a sing-song voice, waving furiously at Nikhil. His hand froze, wavering over the oddly shaped container he was in the process of opening. Nandini skipped up to his table, a suspiciously large smile plastered on her face. He frowned, glancing dubiously at the abnormally sweet-looking fourteen-year-old.

'Nandini...' He greeted her back, stretching out the last syllable of her name.

'*Arrey!* Why are you getting so scared? I just wanted to talk to you!' Nandini attempted to feign innocence, failing miserably at it. Her poor acting skills, combined with the fact that Nikhil had known her since she was three, made it obvious that she had an ulterior motive.

'What about?' he asked, his brows furrowed even further.

'About your trip to Benaras, of course!'

Nikhil had returned from Benaras the previous night. He had gone there on official *Congress* business a week ago. He'd gone so suddenly that not even Maya had a clue about the purpose of his trip.

'Well, it was...an interesting experience...'

Nandini lifted an eyebrow, her hands on her hips, staring sceptically at Nikhil.

'What do you want me to say, Nandu? It was quite nice, I suppose...'

'What did you do there?'

'We...protested.'

Nikhil finished off lamely, making it apparent that he was trying to keep something confidential.

'Bhaiya...' Nandini muttered in a slightly threatening tone. Nikhil knew what came next—a pout followed by angry, boisterous accusations of disloyalty. He wasn't the only drama queen in Chandni Chowk.

'Well, we tried to encourage people to join our fight and pledged to continue our struggle for freedom. And we protested, and hoisted the Indian flag on public buildings. Nothing much apart from that,' Nikhil said it so casually, as if it wasn't a big deal at all.

'Nothing *much!* That's a lot! And to think you would have stopped at *it was an interesting experience*,' Nandini grumbled, folding her arms across her chest, scowling. Why was everyone unwilling to tell her what was going on in the Congress?

'Well, you should have told me what you wanted to hear...' Nikhil replied, defensively.

'I wanted to know what *official business* it was that you went on. And...you wouldn't happen to know whether there would be any future protests similar to the ones that took place in Benaras, would you?'

The second part of her sentence was uttered a little too quickly, the words blending together, almost incomprehensible to any sensible person. Fortunately for Nandini, Nikhil was *not* a sensible person, and had spent far too much time in her company to even pretend to misunderstand her.

'Ah...I see...so my presumption *was* correct,' he tut-tutted loudly, shaking his head, amused at Nandini's desperation.

'What presumption?'

'That you wanted something out of me...'

'No, bhaiya. I was wondering, just like that.'

Nandini swayed from side to side, her arms clasped together, behind her back.

'Yes, of course, *just like that.*' Nikhil's tongue was laced in sarcasm causing Nandini to immediately stop swaying.

'Why don't you believe me? Babu*ji* doesn't believe me either. I'm being honest.'

'All right Nandini, if you insist, then fine. But I don't have time right now. I have...an appointment,' he said rather uncomfortably, as if the thought itself caused him pain.

'I'll come!' Nandini offered, presuming that her offer would be accepted.

'No,' Nikhil replied flatly.

'But why?' Nandini whined. She stopped for a second, as she realised she had been cribbing a lot lately. Oh well, whining was a very useful weapon when it came to dealing with people who were still convinced she was a toddler. That was why she liked spending time with David. He most certainly did not treat her like a child.

'Because it's dangerous,' Nikhil replied.

'Please bhaiya! Don't you start as well!' Nandini complained, knitting her brows together.

'Don't start what?' Nikhil asked, genuinely confused.

'Babu*ji* says the same thing when I deliver his letters to him.'

'Oh, so you've started delivering the letters...'

Once again, Nikhil mumbled to himself, as if whispering to an accomplice. Nandini edged away from him, deeply suspicions about his mental stability.

'Yes...do you know anything about them?' she asked, trying to keep calm, and pretend that she didn't think he was going insane.

'No, nothing apart from the fact that there are some letters being exchanged between your father and some other members of the Congress,' he shrugged, evidently not finding the mention of the letters very important.

'Oh, all right then,' Nandini tried not to sound disappointed, too disappointed, and failing, yet again.

'Well, now when you are convinced that I know nothing, can I go to my appointment?' Nikhil asked teasing. His eyes twinkled mischievously.

'I still want to go with you. I'm not going to change my mind just because you don't know anything about the letters,' Nandini retorted, glaring at him so fiercely that he was afraid to say no.

'All right, but listen, you have to be really quiet. Don't tell your father otherwise he'll be really upset.'

He gave Nandini a very severe look and said, 'And, do as you're told.' Nandini nodded, mock-saluting him. He shifted his gaze, placing the half-open container on the table. Nandini glanced at it briefly, before Nikhil pulled her away.

~

'Nandini, this is my friend and partner, Karamchand.'

Nikhil gestured to a tall, muscular man with a moustache. He appeared to be Nikhil's age, although Nandini couldn't be certain.

'Hello,' Nandini smiled, folding her hands together to greet him.

The man's moustache twitched, as he frowned disapprovingly at Nandini. To him, the presence of a little girl was an unnecessary distraction. It was their responsibility to take care of her, and he neither had the patience, nor the inclination to do so.

'Why did you bring her?' he asked, ignoring Nandini and talking directly to Nikhil. Nandini lowered her gaze, biting her tongue so as not to blurt out something spiteful. She had promised Nikhil that she would not do anything stupid or say anything out of turn.

'We can trust her,' Nikhil wrapped his arm around Nandini's right shoulder, clutching it protectively.

'She needs to leave. We had an agreement.'

The man was still completely unwilling to acknowledge Nandini's presence. Nikhil could sense the muscles in Nandini's shoulders tensing up. He squeezed her thin frame comfortingly, hoping it would keep her anger at bay.

'Listen, I told you we can trust her. She's...'

'I don't care what you say. Do you see *me* bringing little girls along? I thought you understood. This isn't child's play. She needs to leave,' Karamchand repeated himself, and Nandini could have sworn that she saw the muscles in his forehead contract. What a foul, incorrigible, patronising fool! Nandini was biting her tongue so hard she was sure it would start bleeding soon. She felt Nikhil squeeze her shoulder again, and directed her anger toward the street, glowering at the sidewalk.

'Look, we're wasting our time, let's just do what we came here for,' Nikhil was curt, and Nandini could tell he was controlling himself as well. He gestured toward the police station a few metres away, as Karamchand sighed restrainedly.

Nandini frowned, now utterly befuddled. Why had Nikhil just pointed to a police station? Did he have an appointment with the police constable there? Had they come here to lodge a complaint? If so, why was her presence so unwanted by the other man?

'We *are* wasting our time. Tell her to leave or...'

'For God's sake! We can *trust* her! She's Sharma*ji*'s daughter!' Nikhil flared up at Karamchand, abandoning all the self control he had been practising all this while. Much to Nandini's surprise, the man's countenance immediately changed at the mention of her father.

'Oh...all right then...,' he mumbled, suddenly becoming conscious of Nandini's presence there.

'It's very nice to meet you.'

He smiled with a great deal of effort, as if the gesture was causing him terrible physical pain. It would take a lot more than the display of paan-stained teeth to get in Nandini's good books.

'All right, can we just get to work now?' Nikhil asked, breaking the painfully aching silence that was engulfing them. The man shifted his focus from Nandini to Nikhil, and nodded.

'Great. Nandu, since you insisted to come along, you might as well help.'

'Good, I want to help.'

'All right, listen. You have to go inside the police station and make up a story about an accident to the constable there. Say your parents got hurt or something broke...say *anything* to get him distracted.' Nikhil had bent down on his knees to be on level with Nandini. His hands were placed on her shoulders. Nandini was listening attentively to each and every word of his, as if her life depended on it.

'And when you hear a bicycle bell ring three times, just leave the station, okay?' he paused, holding out his hand in front of the moustached man. The man handed him a folded piece of cloth with stripes of white, green and orange sticking out. Nandini pursed her lips, trying to recall where she had seen that design before.

'That's not...is it? It *is!*' Nandini gasped, and her eyes lit up as she remembered exactly where she had seen the pattern.

'The flag? Yes...it is.' Nikhil answered her question, casually. He was beginning to enjoy this.

'So you're going to...'

'Hoist the flag at the police station.'

This time, the moustache man replied, his tone shockingly gentle. Nandini tried to pretend to be nonchalant about the whole affair, but ended up jumping up and down, clapping her hands like the little girl she loathed to be called.

'Oh my God! That is unbelievable!' she squealed, receiving perturbed looks from both Nikhil and the *moustache man*.

'Yes, now calm down and go inside the police station. Please, try *not* to squeal, because, remember, you're going inside the police station to report an accident.' Nandini nodded, perhaps bobbing her head too vigorously, as Nikhil clutched his face in his hands, groaning. Perhaps this hadn't been such a good idea after all.

'Bhaiya, don't worry, I won't act like an idiot inside. I promise.'

Although her words were meant to be reassuring, it didn't ease Nikhil's anxiety. Concerned as he was, he had no choice but to let Nandini go ahead, as they couldn't afford to waste more time. The constable was more likely to believe a small girl anyway.

'Fine. Just go inside and wait for our signal.'

~

With a deep breath, and closed eyes, Nandini entered the police station. When she opened her eyes, she was surprised to see how barren the station seemed. The only things in the room were two tables set up against the wall. Two men were sipping tea in cups made out of clay, looking quite bored. Nandini heaved a sigh of relief. This was it—her chance to be a part of the movement that her parents and friends were so deeply involved in.

'Bhaiyaji! HELP!'

One of the men looked up, narrowing his eyes at Nandini's petite frame. He was in no mood to help a hysterical child.

'What is it?' he snapped, placing his clay cup on the table.

'Bhaiyaji, I need your help!' Nandini said, enlarging her eyes in fear, flailing her hands wildly for extra measure. Needless to say, she took refuge in her over-the-top gestures when struggling to act convincing. It wasn't always the best tactic.

'We heard you the first time. What is it that you need help with?'

The other policeman turned around, rolling his eyes, blatantly irritated with this overtly expressive fourteen-year-old.

'It's...,' she ran to their table, almost sure that by the time she reached, she would have concocted the rest of the story.

'It's...What?'

The first policeman asked shifting a bit in his seat as Nandini came to stand near him. He did not like the proximity between the dramatic child and him. Perhaps, he was merely protecting his cup of tea from Nandini's flailing arms, and he *did* move the cup away from her.

'It is my brother! He...he got hurt!'

She mentally smacked herself for her lack of originality.

'So, go to the hospital, why have you come to us?' the other policeman retorted, sharing a smirk with his colleague before picking up his cup of tea.

'No! You don't understand!' Nandini exclaimed, wild desperation leaking into her voice. The policemen paused for a moment, feeling sympathy for the frenzied child. She had clearly gone insane after seeing her brother hurt, if she hadn't already been before.

'Listen beta, we're sorry, but this is a police station. We can't help you if your brother is hurt.'

The policeman, who had earlier narrowed his eyes at her, now patted her shoulder awkwardly trying to be comforting.

'No, but...' Nandini faltered, staring blankly at the policeman. Her brain was being incredibly slow and uncooperative. Not a single helpful thought had been spewed out. There was only one other thing she could to distract the policemen. She screwed her eyes together. The policemen stared at her, struggling to study the expression on her face.

'What is she...'

Nandini opened her eyes and started wailing loudly without warning. The policemen's mouths fell open, and they gaped as big, fat tears came streaming down her face. She smirked inwardly, as the two men started panicking, terrified of her bawling. *It worked like a charm every time.*

She had learnt this trick very early on in life. Whenever she wanted something done from an older person, excluding her grandmother, all she needed to do was screw her eyes together and start howling. Tears always terrified grown-ups and it was a well-known fact among the children in her neighbourhood.

'Oh no...don't cry, beta. It'll be all right. Your brother will be fine...'

One of the policemen—Nandini couldn't remember which one it was—patted her on her head. She couldn't quite understand why he thought patting her like a dog would soothe and calm her raging nerves. At his touch, she started howling even louder, roughly wiping her cheek, smearing her tears.

'*Baldev!* Get up and let her sit!'

The other constable barked at his colleague. Immediately, the man shot out of his chair, pulling it up for Nandini. Biting her lip to stop herself from laughing, Nandini thanked the man and sat down.

'Would you like anything to eat or drink?' the policeman gently asked Nandini. He had folded his hands together and placed them on the table in front of him. He was peering at her across the table with paternal concern.

'No...thank you...,' she sniffed.

'Are you sure?'

'Yes...I'm just...,' she sniffed again, fumbling with her fingers, looking extremely distressed.

'I understand...*Baldev!* Get her a cup of tea!' He snapped at his employee, who instantly scrambled out of the room through a door that Nandini hadn't even noticed before. As he left, the constable turned and smiled at Nandini.

'I understand you must be distressed. It's very normal, after all, seeing your brother like that...' he spoke to her as if she were broken—not quite right in the head. It was starting to get on Nandini's nerves.

'Yes...it is...,' her words were interrupted by a very loud bicycle bell. It rang thrice, as promised.

'But you're probably right. This is a police station, not a hospital.'

She got up from her seat abruptly, nearly knocking the chair over in her rushed exit.

'I'm sorry for wasting your time. I'd best be going.'

She smiled briefly, and turning around, nearly sprinted out before the constable could react.

On her way out, she saw Nikhil leaning against the bicycle.

'Nikhil, let's go?'

The moustached man's statement came out more as a question than a command. Perhaps he was trying to make up for the rudeness before.

'All done?' Nandini asked, surprised that they had finished so quickly. At least, to her, it had seemed like a fairly quick process. She had begun enjoying her charade. It was nice to see grown men run around just to stop her from crying.

'Yes...are you disappointed?' Nikhil teased her. Nandini retorted by sticking her tongue out at him, and shoving him playfully.

'All right, let's go now,' the moustached man said, glancing nervously at the police station.

Nandini refrained from rolling her eyes at him. She didn't understand why he was getting paranoid. She was quite certain that if the policemen hadn't come looking for after her abrupt exit, they wouldn't bother now. Then again, one could never be too sure.

Nikhil moved away from the bicycle, and the moustached man walked up to it. It was clearly too small for him. He looked like a giant on it. He smiled and waved at Nikhil and Nandini, and turned the bicycle around. Nandini fought back her laughter as the man pedalled away, his bottom hanging off the seat.

'It's not nice to laugh, Nandu...' Nikhil scolded, his voice breaking at the end of the sentence as he burst into laughter himself.

'Yes, of course,' Nandini replied sarcastically, and Nikhil nudged her to keep quiet. Laughing, the two started making their way back to Chandni Chowk.

Behind them, on a flagpole atop the police station, a tri-coloured flag swayed with the wind. Later on in the day, passers-by would notice that it wasn't a British flag. The flag had stripes of orange, white and green, and if you looked close, you could see a blue spinning wheel right in the middle of the flag.

The police station would be informed, but the constable would not budge from his seat, and continue sipping tea instead. Much later in the day, a British official would visit and reprimand the Indian policemen for not taking the flag off. The official would then be asked to burn it amid a bunch of confused onlookers. It might have been a mere piece of cloth, but to the nervous constable, it was a symbol—of rebellion, growing agitation and the crumbling British Empire.

It was the *Swaraj* flag.

18

Ranchi, 2011

'You really cried in front of a policeman?' I asked my grandma, staring at her mouth agape for an abnormally long time. It must have made her really uncomfortable. She told me to close my mouth and look away.

'Yes...' my grandma replied a little wearily, probably relieved that I had regained my composure.

'And you really participated in the protests and delivered letters from the Congress to your dad?'

'Oh yes.'

'And you helped the other comrades hoist the flag at police station?'

'Yes...' my grandma nodded, and I could tell that she was amused, a smile playing on her lips.

'I guess I was wrong...' I muttered, shaking my head, as my grandma looked at me questioningly. Grinning, I sort of came to agree—

'I guess history *can* be cool.'

She grinned back at me and for a moment I could imagine her transforming into the little mischievous, but brave, Nandini she had been years ago. I could picture her running around delivering letters, crying in front of the policemen, stirring up a rebellion. I could see her risking her life, inspired by Nehru's words; and then it suddenly struck me.

'Naani, wasn't all this dangerous?' I asked. As soon as I said it, she sat upright, her eyes glinting violently with what I could only think of as pride.

'No, not very much,' she replied airily.

'But you could have been arrested, or beaten up, right?'

'Well yes, but I wasn't. I was alert and cautious at all times.'

I bit my lip thoughtfully, and my grandma prodded me, asking if everything was all right. I shook my head, but it still bothered me—the thought that my grandma and countless other children (probably my age) had been fighting for a cause without bothering much about their own lives. They could have been imprisoned. They could have been beaten up. *Why did they endanger their lives?*

'Was it worth it?' I asked out loud, more to myself than to my grandma.

'Of course, it was. *Freedom always is.*'

19

Wilson House, New Delhi, February 1943

David returned home after a particularly enjoyable day with Maya and Nandini at Chandni Chowk. Maya had dropped him home and left in a hurry. She had to take her mother to the hospital, yet again. David was beginning to get slightly worried about Maya's mother; she seemed to be going to the hospital an awful lot. He wasn't the only one who appeared to be worried. While Maya was perfectly calm, waving off his concern saying her mother was quite old, Nandini seemed just as anxious, if not more, than David. He could tell by how absent-minded Nandini had become, often not responding to him, and wandering off without waiting for him to follow her. Home had become a buffer zone for him—from the malice and anxiety that inundated Chandni Chowk.

'Ah, there you are David. Excellent!'

He smiled politely at his mother, who walked over to him with a glass of white wine in her hand. He pursed his lips, feigning disapproval as he stared pointedly at the glass in her hand.

'Isn't it a bit early for you to start drinking, mother?' David mocked her good-humouredly, grinning impishly. Much to his surprise, he received a smack on his head, rather than a bout of the girlish giggles he was expecting from her.

'That's not the way to talk to your mother,' she scolded him. David blinked dumbly, surprised by the sudden harshness in her tone. Never had his parents scolded him, barring ayah*ji*'s occasional reprimands. His parents had always laughed good-naturedly at his antics, and left much of the disciplining to his ayah. He was expected to be polite in front of guests, but when it was just his parents, the rules were relaxed. Of course, there were guests at the Wilson house almost every day.

'Is something wrong?' David asked, now genuinely concerned about his mother. He didn't spend a lot of time with his mother, so he wasn't sure if the frown lines on her forehead were a recent development or not. She certainly did seem older than before.

'Oh, yes, of course. I'm fine,' she replied, entirely blasé all of a sudden. Before he could say anything else, she pulled him by his arm inside the living room.

'Mr Morris is here to take your measurements,' she gestured to a short, balding man. He had a whiskery moustache, like an old hairbrush was stuck to his upper lip. A measuring tape was hanging limply from his protruding stomach.

'But why?' David asked, frowning. He had bought clothes just a month ago, and in his opinion, he most definitely did not need new ones. He hated getting measured for clothes. It was boring and a waste of time. He wanted to do something much more entertaining.

'Because you need some British clothes,' his mother replied, pushing him forward, closer to Mr Morris.

'But I don't...'

'You're getting *English* clothes, David,' his mother said firmly. Once again, David was surprised at her aggressive reaction. Mr Morris instructed him to hold out his right arm.

'But why, I don't really...'

'Dear God! Child! For once, do what you're being told to without asking a million questions!' his mother exclaimed, the wine glass in her hand shaking violently. David exchanged a half-terrified, half-concerned look with Mr Morris, who seemed to be as scared as David was.

'On second thoughts, British clothes sound perfectly fine to me,' David said quietly. His mother walked over to the bar, pouring some wine in her glass.

'Don't worry, son. This has been happening with a lot of British couples recently. Your parents are no exception,' Mr Morris muttered, noting down the length of David's right arm.

'What?' David asked, bewildered by both Mr Morris's comment and his mother's behaviour.

'After those Indians resigned, everyone's been a bit edgy. Turn a little to the side, please.' David obliged. His mother was keeping a keen eye on him from the bar.

'Which Indians...resigned from what?' David asked, whispering, in the hope that his mother wouldn't hear. She seemed a little preoccupied with her drink. Mr Morris spread the tape across the length of his leg.

He tried to ignore the squirmy feeling in his stomach, as if he was going to be sick.. He didn't like the idea of someone measuring him with an inch-tape, wrapping it around his chest, legs and arms. To him, if felt like a gross invasion of privacy.

'Those Indians...*ah*, I can't remember their names,' Mr Morris sighed, pausing between his ritual of taking a note of the measurements. He removed the inch-tape from David's leg, clutching it tightly perhaps hoping to squeeze out the names from his brain.

'Well, what did they resign from?' David asked in an attempt at being helpful.

'From the Viceroy's Council, their names will come to me...'

'You mean the Viceroy's *Executive* Council?' David bit his tongue, mentally slapping himself for correcting the man. He had been told on several occasions by Maya that it was rude to correct people, especially those who were older than him.. He couldn't help it; he was a stickler for details. Fortunately for him, Mr Morris didn't seem to mind.

'Yes them...*ah*! I remember!'

'Who?' David asked eagerly, which was rather strange, as there was a slim chance he would know any names of the Council members, let alone the Indian ones.

'M.S. Aney, N.R Sarkar and H.D...No HP... *Ah*, I can't remember, H *something* Modi.'

'*Ah*, I see...' David said politely, realising the knowledge of their names served no purpose. It wasn't like he knew them personally. They were just names. If he saw them in the paper, he wouldn't feel any emotional attachment to them. He might not even question their dismissal.

'Yes, I didn't know they existed before this incident, to tell you the truth,' Mr Morris confessed, resuming his abandoned activity of measuring David for his clothes. For a while, David stood motionless, listening to the rustle of his clothes and the scratching of Mr Morris's pen. His mother slurped at her wine loudly, and David was sure it wasn't her first, or second glass.

'So...why does their resignation put everyone on edge? That is, if no one knew about them before, it shouldn't pose a problem for anybody, right?' David asked, breaking the silence.

'Because they're *Indian*, aren't they?' Mr Morris replied, as if it was the most obvious thing in the world.

'So what?' David interjected, perhaps a tad bit defensive.

Ever since he had become good friends with Nandini, he had become slightly possessive of the *Indians*. Whenever there was a party at his house, and he sensed the conversation taking a turn toward criticising Indian people, he would leave the room, for fear of overstepping his well drawn out boundaries. The Indian bashing had been happening more and more recently.

It wasn't that he didn't like Indians before he met Nandini, but he didn't *know* much about them earlier. The only opinion he had formed about Indians was based on the information given to him by Maya, but that wasn't enough for him to defend them. His time at Chandni Chowk had made him more vocal in discussions with his guests. He realised that he was the only one who had actually interacted with Indian people in a normal situation, and every prejudiced thing that the others said made his blood boil.

'So, you haven't heard anything? Don't you read the news, son?'

'Not really, what happened?' David tried to mask his irritation at Mr Morris's surprise. He wasn't a big fan of politics anyway. Of course, he knew about the protests, and the bridges burning, but not much beyond that. He felt like getting involved would mean he would have to choose a side, and he wasn't ready for that.

'The Indian civil servants have been acting up a lot recently. Since August, they started showing preference for the Congress. Students have started going on strikes, and I'm sure you've heard about the protests and the bridges?'

'Yes, I have.'

'Well, that and the flag...the *Swaraj* flag. A lot of the students and members of the Congress have somehow managed to hoist the flag from post offices, police stations, railway stations, telegraph poles.....anything they can get their hand on really.'

'Really!' David couldn't help but be hurt. His best friend lived in a family and a neighbourhood that was thriving with freedom fighters. She had participated in protests herself. He was miffed that she hadn't even bothered to inform him about the flag hoistings and bridge burnings. He knew for a fact that her father was an active member of the Congress, and that her mother too participated in the protests.

'Yes, that's why your mother, like several other British mothers, is rather frazzled,' Mr Morris explained, patting him on the back before asking him to turn around and placing the tape across his shoulders.

'But why is she insisting on getting me English clothes?' David asked, realising only after the words escaped his mouth, that Mr Morris would probably not have an answer to that. How could he? He was neither a woman, nor a friend of David's mother.

'Because she doesn't want to flaunt her love for India. when you have to prove that you're British enough for the government.' Mr Morris scribbled down the length of David's shoulders. David had to admit, he was quite impressed with Mr Morris's ability to multitask.

'But *we're* not the government,' David argued, wondering exactly why he was arguing with a tailor about his mother's sudden desire to get him to be the perfect English gentleman—something he truly wasn't.

'But you're British,' the man said simply, stretching out his inch-tape, sizing David up, and possibly contemplating which body part to measure next.

'Yes, but...'

'May I have you turn a little toward me, please,' he requested, placing the inch-tape across David's chest.

'Listen, my guess is that they probably don't want to favour the Indians. After all, the *Indian* civil servants have made it clear where their loyalties stand. So if we support them, then we'll most definitely be labelled as outcasts within English society and the government,' Mr Morris paused before writing down the new set of measurements on his notepad. David remained silent for a few minutes, trying to process the tailor's words.

'*Ah*...I see...' he finally spoke, still mulling over what had been said.

He wasn't completely convinced by Mr Morris's explanation. He knew that it would be very dangerous to talk to his mother about this subject. His father had gone to England on some "business". David had thought that the way he had said it was really suspicious, as if the business entailed something more than paperwork and dinners. He wondered if it had anything to do with the sudden resignations, and the way his mother was behaving.

~

'So, why are we at this sweet shop again? Isn't this where that man had insulted me?' David asked, as Nandini walked over to him with a cup of tea.

'Because Pandit*ji* is going to give a speech which we can hear on the radio. The shop owner won't even notice you,' she slurped loudly at her tea, closing her eyes to savour the flavour.

'Oh. The famous Panditji. This should be exciting.' David rolled out the last word as Nandini scowled darkly at him. She knew he was mocking her, because he considered her fascination with Nehru a little extreme, only because he didn't know. He didn't understand how inspiring a leader Nehru was. His words were enough to instil courage—a fire, a passion and desire for change in thousands of people.

'You'll see...' Nandini grumbled.

The crackling white noise from the radio drifted toward the pair, as they sat, sipping their tea. Nandini turned toward the noise with a wide smile on her face. She elbowed David, and groaning loudly, he turned toward her.

'What!' he hissed, as Nandini put a finger on her lips, asking him to keep quiet. Panditji was on air.

A healthy society must have the seeds of revolt in it. It must alternate between revolution and consideration.

David had to keep himself from bursting into laughter at the sight of Nandini. She was listening to the garbled speech with rapt attention, as if every jumbled word of the speech were pure gold. David was almost certain that she was holding her breath in.

'Wow Nandu. You're right. He is brilliant,' he mocked her. She swatted at him, and he expertly avoided her. He had become quite experienced in thwarting Nandini's wrath. David decided to remain quiet and actually listen. After all, it was important to his friend.

It is the function of youth to supply this dynamic element in society; to be the standard bearers in revolt against all that is evil and to prevent older people from suppressing all social progress and movement by the mere weight of their inertia.

Nandini gave David a look, which made him purse his lips in annoyance. She knew that she had been right. She could see it in his face—the same awe-inspiring energy. The very same fuel for change, and a desire to do something of significance. She had succeeded in her mission. David had realised the power of Nehru.

Reject utterly what I say to you if you think it is wrong. But reject also everything, however hallowed it may be by tradition and convention and religious sanction, if your reason tells you that it is wrong or unsuited to the present condition.

Nandini slurped her tea, throwing a furtive sideway-glance at her friend. He kept quiet, staring into his cup of tea, waiting for her to say something.

'Well?' Nandini asked, almost inaudibly.

'Yes,' he replied, through clenched teeth. Her smugness was thoroughly irritating, because they both knew she was absolutely right.

'Yes what?' she asked, and he could tell that she was smirking. He still avoided her scrutinising gaze.

'Yes, he's brilliant,' he replied monotonously, and Nandini's face split into one of her gigantic smiles. He truly did think that Nehru's speech was magnificent. At a time when everyone was desperately trying to cling to traditions—be it his own mother or the sweet shop owner—the speech was a clarion call for change. It was a call for the young, for people like Nandini and David, who believed in equality and freedom for all, to come forward and fight for what is *right* and *just*.

'See. Now you're completely *Indian*. You drink chai from our stalls; you are almost a *gilli danda* champion and now a fan of *Panditji*.'

'I suppose I am,' David replied, wondering if that was all it took to be *Indian*.

Was only the desire for change enough to turn Indian?

~

'So, why did they resign?' Nandini asked her father again, as he took another sip of water. The recent resignations were all that the neighbourhood had talked about for days.

'I wouldn't know for sure, because I don't know them personally, but I think it is in protest of Gandhi*ji*'s imprisonment,' Vikas Sharma replied, taking a bite of his food.

'But why now? He was imprisoned last year, in August. Why...' Nandini counted the number of months that had passed since Gandhi's imprisonment.

'Why are they resigning five months later?'

'Well, ever since Gandhi*ji* began fasting, there have been more protests than before. Didn't you notice the strikes outside schools?'

Nandini nodded, confirming she had seen the crowd of college students rallying outside her school and other places around Delhi.

'Well, there have been rumours that the government has already made arrangements for Gandhi*ji*'s funeral, so everyone's turned hostile and anti-government. People have been crowding outside the Aga Khan Palace in Poona where Gandhi*ji* is imprisoned, and...'

'And the Indian members of the Viceroy's Executive Council have resigned to express *their* resentment toward the government's way of handling things.' It made sense all of a sudden. The resignations, which seemed out of the blue, were a sign of protest—toward the unfairness that the country's national symbol of peace and unity was being treated with.

'Yes, exactly.' Vikas nodded, pleased that his daughter had understood.

'But, I don't understand, why is Gandhi*ji* fasting?' Nandini asked, after a brief silence. Her father chewed on his food, looking in the distance as if in deep thought.

'Nandu, all these questions that you're asking me, I don't have definite answers for. I can only guess from what I know,' he replied, swallowing his food.

'Well, what's your guess?' Nandini pressed on. Her keenness in politics motivated her to put things in perspective. Of course, she had always been interested in the events taking place in the country, thanks to her unconditional respect and admiration for one leader—Nehru. It wasn't until she personally joined the protests, flag hoistings and letter deliveries that she started really caring about what happened to the country. She felt like she had a hand in shaping its future, and if anyone tampered with her vision, it bothered her a lot.

'I've heard that it is against the government. He was apparently asked to condemn the violence…'

'What violence?' Nandini interrupted.

'The…burning of the bridges and the riots happening in and around the country. Anyway, he was asked to put an end to them, but he said he wouldn't.'

'Why? Isn't he always telling us to adopt non-violence?'

'Yes, but he's holding the government responsible for the outbreak of violence. He has argued that the government's rather draconian methods and detention of thousands of

Congressmen have only worked toward provoking the people of the country.'

'Really? I thought only the big leaders have been imprisoned.'

'No, many Congressmen have been put behind bars. That's why...' Vikas faltered, an expression of panic on his face, like he'd been caught in the act. Nandini stared at her father, concerned. A part of her hoped that he would tell her what she had been yearning to hear—the secrets he refused to share. Much to her disappointment, her father continued, 'That's why Gandhiji's fasting for twenty-one days,' he concluded, his words tumbling out somewhat hastily.

'But then...how come you're not in prison?'

Nandini's father raised his eyebrows questioningly at her, and she blushed, suddenly aware of what she had just blurted out without much thought. Of course she didn't want her father to be in prison. It had been an innocent question!

'No, what I mean is that...'

'I understand what you mean. Yes Nandu, it might seem like I'm a big part of the Congress, but in reality, I'm only a drop in the ocean.'

'But even then... If you're organising all these rallies and demonstrations, then how is the government not...well...how are they not *aware* of you?' Nandini struggled to come out with a delicate way to communicate what she had hastened with moments ago. She was quite sure she had managed.

Her father sighed, appearing quite exhausted with the conversation. He seemed to be tiring of conversations with Nandini quite often since the last couple of months. Perhaps his work with the Congress and the school were taking a toll on him. After all, he wasn't the youngest or the fittest member.

'But I'm not the only one, Nandu. It's because I'm your father, and since Nikhil and I are the only members of Congress that you know, you feel as if we work a lot, and are the most indispensable members of the Party. There are other people who play much bigger roles than us, who fill in the shoes of Nehru and Patel...'

Nandini was thoroughly convinced that her father was merely being humble. He had a knack of taking compliments and turning them around to make his accomplishments seem trivial. Most of the time, it irritated Nandini immensely. There were several occasions when she had begged her father to accept a compliment. He had not.

'But babu*ji*, when I met someone else from the Party with Nikhil bhaiya the other day, he seemed to be in awe of you,' Nandini insisted, her eyes twinkling, confident that she would persuade her father to believe in his own merit for once.

'When did you meet another member of the Party?' her father asked, curious. Nikhil hadn't told him about any such meeting. Usually, Nikhil would tell him everything concerning Nandini, especially when she was with that British boy. Vikas had requested Nikhil to keep an eye on their friendship, not that he wanted to spy on them. He simply wanted to keep a keen eye on the boy, just in case he hurt his daughter again.

'Oh! Nikhil bhaiya took me to...' she stopped midway. Her face was painted with a similar expression of panic as her father's had been only a few minutes ago.

'Where did he take you?' he asked, perhaps his tone a little too harsh, as Nandini flinched.

'No...just...*he-took-me-with-him-to-hoist-the-flag.*'

She spoke in one breath, making it extremely difficult for her father to understand exactly *where* Nikhil had taken her. He normally wouldn't have been so concerned, as Nikhil was quite trustworthy, but Nandini's sudden trepidation was definitely a bad sign.

'Where?' he pressed on, staring firmly at Nandini with his beady, black eyes. She gulped, deciding that she had no choice but to tell him.

'He took me with him to a police station. He...he hoisted the *Swaraj* flag there with the help of a tall man with a moustache.'

She dropped her gaze, staring intently at the floor, a habit she took refuge in whenever she got into an argument with her father, or was afraid of what was to come next.

'He did *what*? With *who*?' her father exclaimed, and she could hear his voice shaking with anger. She bit her lip nervously, hoping dearly that Nikhil wouldn't get into trouble because of her big mouth.

'I...I didn't know the man's name, but he had a moustache,' Nandini mumbled, now twiddling with her thumbs.

'I can't believe he would take you...with *Karamchand* of all people!' her father muttered.

'Don't get upset with Nikhil bhaiya, please,' Nandini pleaded meekly. Her father was frowning furiously at the half-empty steel plate placed in front of him, possibly imagining it to be Nikhil's face.

'Nandini, whether I get upset with Nikhil or not is not under your control. What he did was...' her father shook his head, unable to come up with a word strong enough for the horrifying *sin* that Nikhil had committed.

'But babu*ji*, it is not that terrible. Nothing happened. We weren't hurt, and no one tried to hurt us either,' Nandini tried to explain that the situation wasn't as serious as her paranoid father was making it out to be. She wasn't ready to factor in that Vikas, being a father, was bound to be irrationally protective of his little girl.

'Do you have any idea of what *could* have happened? It is not child's play Nandini, people have got hurt before,' her father said, trying to keep calm and be patient. Clearly, he was failing.

'Yes, but we *didn't*. Bhaiya made sure that there was no possibility of me getting hurt, and...'

'You can never make sure that you don't get hurt, Nandini, unless you stay away from these things.'

'But I don't understand what the big problem is. You let me participate in the protest, didn't you? And the old man got hurt there, didn't he?'

'Yes, but there were more *people* there. And more importantly, *I* was there.'

'Yes, but you were leading from the front. If I'd got hurt, you wouldn't even have found out.'

'Yes, but...' her father sighed, struggling with the ongoing argument. He wasn't sure how to explain the situation to his daughter. He didn't know what exactly perturbed him so much about the entire incident. Lots of children went with their siblings or friends and hoisted flags on top of public buildings. How many times had he seen little children, perhaps even younger than Nandini, rallying around the city, fasting and openly revolting against the British? But Nandini was his daughter, and he wouldn't let her come near danger. He remembered bailing out many children from prison. He didn't want Nandini to go near any of that. She was far too young, far too innocent.

'I was keeping an eye on you. If *anything* were to happen to you, I would have been informed within seconds,' her father lied blatantly. He had certainly not been keeping an eye on her. In fact, she was the last thing on his mind the day of the protest. The responsibility of ensuring that the protest went smoothly had preoccupied his mind to an extent that he hardly had room for anything else. Guilt-ridden, he realised his daughter was right.

'But...' Nandini faltered, now completely stumped. How was she to respond to *that*?

'But even then, you couldn't have been sure that *nothing* would happen to me...'

'Yes, but I would have been able to take care of you if something *did*. And with Nikhil, it was different. It was just you, Nikhil and Karamchand. And Karamchand can be quite dangerous,' he tried reassuring himself, more than her. He had been irresponsible and selfish. There was no excuse for his behaviour.

Things were going to change from now. Nandini's safety would assume priority, even if it meant compromising on his position in the Party. She was the most important part of his life, and even the thought of her in danger made his stomach churn.

'Really? What does he do?' Nandini asked, momentarily distracted from their debate.

'It doesn't matter what he does,' he dismissed her question, as usual. He trusted her to deliver letters but not with his colleagues and friends. She realised that it would be futile to press the issue, so decided to change the topic.

'But why is it such a problem? Children participate in rallies and revolts against the British all the time!' Nandini exclaimed, voicing what her father had been wondering a moment ago.

'Yes, but they're not *my* daughters,' Vikas retorted almost immediately. Nandini opened her mouth, and failing to formulate words, promptly closed it.

'That's it then, isn't it?' Nandini asked. There was an unmistakeable edge in her voice this time. If the situation weren't so serious, Vikas might have been amused with her daughter's annoyance.

'What is it?' her father prompted her to explain.

'I'm your *daughter*. A girl. So *of* course I shouldn't be allowed to go and do things that are meant for *men* and *boys*.'

This time, there was no mistaking the bitterness and seething rage in her voice.

Her father blinked blankly at her, confused at the turn their debate had taken. Not in a million years would he ever stop his daughter from doing something just because she had long hair and no facial hair. He had made this clear to several people, be it his neighbours, his relatives or his own *mother*. He was a teacher—dedicated to enriching and broadening the minds of youngsters.

'That's not it, Nandu, and you *know* that,' he said, rediscovering his ability to speak gently. He was very hurt by his daughter's accusation. Under all her anger, Nandini knew very well that her father did belong to the group of male *chauvinists*.

'Frankly, I'm shocked that you would even *think* of accusing me like that. You know I'm not so narrow-minded. I wouldn't have let you meet your *firang* friend if I was as terrible as you claim...,' he continued coldly. His distress was slowly being replaced by anger.

Nandini bit her tongue to prevent herself from saying something she would regret later. The topic of her friendship with David invariably brought in tense moments of silence between them. He abhorred the fact that he was British. He simply couldn't understand that it didn't matter to Nandini. She cherished her friendship with him. David had proven to be a good friend and far better company than anyone else in her neighbourhood.

Nandini thought it best to steer the conversation to safer waters.

'What about Ma?'

'What about her?' Nandini's father asked, genuinely confused.

'Is she happy painting slogans, cooking and making Congress badges?'

There was a silence. Vikas stared at his food, opening and closing his mouth like a puppet.

'You…you don't have to worry about that. Are you done with your food? Then go play.'

Nandini bit her tongue so hard she might as well have pierced it. She wanted to scream at her father. Here she was, trying to have a proper, *real* discussion with him, and he was completely unwilling to talk to her. She was most certainly not going to go play. She was going to sit there and force him to talk, even if it made him flap his mouth like a dying fish.

'Well, why else would it concern you so much that I went with Nikhil bhaiya?' Nandini attacked him again where she knew it really hurt. He prided himself on being a liberal father. The idea that he could be anything else disturbed him deeply. She knew it was a cruel thing to do, but the frustration she had kept bottled up for weeks had blurred her compassion.

'Because you're my daughter,' he said simply, as if that was a valid explanation enough. Despite her words—sharp as knives, sour as tamarind, he chose to ignore her cold callousness. He was the adult here, after all. It was time he began acting like one.

'Yes, but…'

'There's absolutely no reason for you to feel that I'm treating you differently because you're a girl. Had it been my son, I would have been equally furious with Nikhil,' her father interrupted, taking another gulp of water.

'I'm not too sure about that, babu*ji*. It seems you would have treated me differently had I *been* a boy.'

'Listen Nandini, I can't convince you to believe me, because you're obviously adamant,' he got up, holding the steel plate of half-eaten food in his hand. He was tired and felt exhausted of arguing with his daughter. He was drained by her countless rebuttals. Why did she expect things to always meet her terms and conditions, wondered her exasperated father. She thought she knew everything, was always right. He'd forgotten what it was like to have a teenager—pulling him from all corners, stretching out his patience till it was as thin as butter he spread on his paranthas. It was wearing him out completely.

'So, I won't waste our time.'

He turned away from his daughter before he could see guilt well up in her eyes. He knew if he saw her sad, he would cave in and apologise. So, without another word or glance in her direction, he stalked away, leaving his daughter more confused and frustrated than before.

20

New Delhi, 1943

The cold war between Nandini and father continued for weeks. It wasn't entirely for lack of trying to sort things out. Vikas was far too busy juggling his school work with his ever increasing list of responsibilities for Congress. Dealing with his obstinate teenage daughter was the last thing on his mind. He missed most family meals, limiting the amount of time he actually spent in Nandini's presence. The rare occasions they were together in a room were spent in stony, uncomfortable silence. He avoided her gaze, studiously glaring at any flat surface in front of him, be it a steel place or their floor.

Nandini wasn't too thrilled with her father, but his silence certainly perturbed her. She would have preferred a good scolding over his aloofness, as if she wasn't even worth his anger. She wasn't tempted to apologise though. She threw herself into the Party activities, with Nikhil serving as her source of information. He had been saved from Vikas' ire as well, and had apparently only been severely reprimanded. Nandini wasn't quite sure what that meant, but Nikhil's limbs still appeared to be intact, so she wasn't much concerned.

Nandini was lucky to have a friend in David. In times when even the Party couldn't distract her from her father's disappointment, constantly looming over her head, David's presence came as a welcome diversion. Their friendship had come a long way. They weren't limited to playing games on the street anymore. Like Nandini, David was becoming increasingly interested in the political scene. Like a sponge, he soaked up any sort of information that Nandini could give him. Nandini was his only source of information. His parents hardly allowed him to sit in on conversations when they discussed politics, claiming he was too "young" to understand. The rare occasions he was allowed were dreadfully boring. The "tea-infused bumbling idiots", as he liked to call them, simply parroted what the British papers wrote. With Nandini, he didn't have to worry about that. She thought a lot, perhaps too much, about every little thing of significance. He wasn't afraid of being 'improper' in front of her and neither was she.

Despite how much he enjoyed spending time with Nandini; David couldn't help but notice that something had definitely changed. It wasn't that she kept things from him. She answered all his questions and argued with him till she was blue in the face and her eyes were ablaze with ferocity. When it came to Party activities though, she did seem a little reserved. David knew that she had been involved in a lot more protests, and she was quite vocal about her dislike of the bridge burnings. Nehru violently opposed it, so, Nandini obviously did too. Every time David mentioned Party activities though, Nandini managed to steer the conversation to books, food or sport. On one occasion, she had stuffed his face with jalebi and bid him a hasty goodbye. Despite her bizarre methods of deflection, David wasn't deterred. He planned to find out just what was going on with his friend.

On a particularly warm day (for March), David went to visit Nandini in Chandni Chowk. Much like most of their conversations, this one had taken a political turn. When he sheepishly asked her about Congress activities, her back instantly stiffened. She started twiddling her thumbs nervously, and he was sure she was going to grab the sweets in front of her and stuff them in his mouth. Much to his surprise, she remained frozen, her eyes trained on his face, guilt welling in her eyes.

'Nandu...' he said her name gently, trying to coax her out of her panicked haze. She blinked her guilt away, and flashed him her trademark smile. He lifted an eyebrow incredulously at her, and the smile instantly slipped off her face.

'I know you think I'm hiding something from you...' she said, her voice almost a whisper. It was his turn to panic. He didn't want to hurt her feelings, but they never lied to each other. Honesty—that was the only thing they had promised each other in their friendship.

'Well...' he tried to sugar-coat the inevitable truth, but it was enough for her to understand.

'You *do*, then?' she asked, almost scoffing. David nodded sheepishly.

'I am *not*,' she huffed, looking away from him. David chuckled. If he hadn't been suspicious before, he was certain now. There was no mistaking it—Nandini was definitely hiding something from him.

'Of course you're not,' he declared, with a mix of sarcasm and bitterness in his voice. He thought she trusted him. Clearly he had been wrong.

'All right, I might be hiding something from you,' she said, sighing. Sometimes, it was incredibly annoying to have a friend who knew her so well.

'Go ahead then...' he had a stupid smug expression on his face, which he knew she found incredibly exasperating.

'Well...'

Nandini told him about the monkey brigade, the letters, the burning of the bridges, the strikes and the fasts. Her voice got louder and louder and her gestures more exaggerated. Her eyes sparkled with excitement as she narrated it all. David had to suppress his laughter as she made her antics seem like a secret agent's mission. He understood what it meant to her, but it could hardly be seriously dangerous. Her father wouldn't have let her do everything she did if it had been otherwise. Then again, her father barely talked to her, so it was quite unlikely he would know everything about Nandini's adventures.

David envied Nandini. He was jealous of the things she was allowed to do, the adventures she could boast about. He itched for a chance to hoist a flag atop a police station, and run around delivering letters. He wished he could share Nandini's feeling of being unreasonably self-important. He wanted to talk about Subhash Chandra Bose and protest like a dedicated revolutionary. He thought it would affect him personally. That is when he realised what Nandini meant when she said that he was actually *Indian* at heart. It was because he *wanted* the things that she had. He wanted it so badly; he pined for it. He ached to be like her. Maybe then it would matter to him as much as it did to her.

'I trust you; I know you won't tell anyone. Even if you're tempted to, please, for the sake of our friendship, don't tell *anyone*,' Nandini said, holding out her hand for him to shake—a promise.

He could never be like *her*. He didn't have the same upbringing, or lifestyle. He lived in a plush bungalow in *Lodhi*

Colony; she lived in a small house in Chandni Chowk. His food was served on an elaborately carved ebony table, and she ate her meals sitting on the floor. He wasn't like *her*, but the least he could do was keep her secrets safe with him.

'I wouldn't even dream of telling anyone,' David solemnly shook her hand. She burst into laughter at his serious expression, and used her free hand to pinch his nose.

'What was that for?' he asked, indignantly.

'Just for fun,' she shrugged, taking another sip of her tea as David looked at her, concerned, yet again, for her mental stability.

21

New Delhi, August 1943

Surprise was a foreign concept to David. With his social interaction limited mostly to adults, he had learned to accept quite early on that excitement could only be faked. The unexpected frightened him to the extent that he dreaded it in any form. He had resisted it when he first met Nandini, but being with her meant that he often had to jump instead of carefully tiptoe into situations. Be it a public fight in Chandni Chowk, or helping an old man while everyone in the neighbourhood chose to silently watch, disapprovingly— he no longer loathed the unknown and unanticipated. His best friend gave him the courage to do what *he* felt was right. She pushed him to think about every little thing he did, which spurred him to form his own opinions. He still wasn't used to having friends around—though people who cared for him in a way different than his parents; those who spent time with him, teased him out of *choice*. People who he fought with, but who would help him without batting an eyelid, without him even asking for it.

When ayah*ji* had invited him over to her house for lunch, the last thing on his mind was a party—a *birthday* party—for *him*. He had nearly forgotten his own birthday, and had definitely not expected ayah*ji* to remember it, let alone throw a surprise party. For *him*.

He hadn't anticipated the wordless, tearful joy he'd feel upon being welcomed with a chorus of *Happy Birthday* as he pushed open ayah*ji*'s heavy wooden door. Amidst all the wishes, and presents received, David barely had time to thank the person who had organised it all.

He waded his way through all the children of the colony who had gathered for his birthday celebration. He was surprised to see them, as they religiously avoided him whenever they saw him. He was certain they had come only to gorge on the *free food*. He didn't mind—the only people who mattered were Maya, Nikhil and Nandini.

He was distracted when Maya approached him and marked his forehead with vermilion. Then, setting the steel plate aside, she signalled Nikhil. He fished something out of his pocket, handing it to her.

'We give money on birthdays, not gifts,' she explained, as she gave David a two-rupee coin. David gasped, and instinctively refused the money. Two rupees was far too big an amount to accept.

'You can't refuse what is given to you by elders. That's wrong,' Maya nearly chastised him, pushing the coin back into his palm. David looked at Nandini, as if seeking an answer. She shrugged at him, offering him no advice or insight. The traitor! David had no choice but to nod, and pocket the gift.

'All right, now let's go and eat,' said Nikhil, rubbing his hands together. He had clearly been waiting patiently for the ritual to finish. Maya chuckled and playfully slapped her brother on the shoulder. Together, they walked out of the room. Nikhil bombarded Maya with a barrage of questions about the menu that had been prepared.

David eyed Nandini. Nandini tilted an eyebrow, her response equally, if not more smug than her friend's.

'You were too lazy to get me a gift, weren't you?' David asked, now grinning at Nandini. The party was more than he could have asked for. He knew Nandini had been the main party-planner. She was the only one who could have convinced all the children in the colony to come.

'I was *not!* I did get you something,' Nandini scoffed, folding her arms across her chest in indignation. David blinked, surprised. He had truly not expected anything. He knew Nandini didn't have much to spend. He often saw her negotiating with the chaiwallas and sweet shop owners to let her pay later. They always acquiesced to her pleas. She had a certain way of scrunching up her face and making her eyes seem doleful at the same time, on the verge of crying. It worked without fail every time.

'What is it?' David asked, getting restless. Nandini sniffed superciliously, sticking her chin in the air.

'Well, you can't have it now. You weren't very nice to me,' she taunted him, fighting the urge to break into a smile, or giggle. David mumbled a meek apology.

'What's that?' Nandini asked, leaning toward David.

'I am truly sorry for my insensitivity. I hope you can forgive me,' he muttered, his head hung in apparent shame.

'You're such an old man, David,' Nandini chuckled. David shook his head, feigning disbelief, but couldn't help smiling himself as he saw the light dancing in Nandini's eyes, her chuckles getting louder.

'All right, now give me my present,' he demanded.

'Please,' he added as an afterthought.

Nandini nodded and reached for her bag, which had been dumped on top of a table. She retrieved a smaller bag from inside, and handed it to David, expressionless. With great exuberance, David flipped the bag upside down and the contents inside fell on his flat palm. It was a concave wooden ball.

For the second time that day, David felt a wave of emotions wash over, nearly drowning him. He tried to muster the words to thank his friend—his very dear friend. Words failed him.

The *gilli* that Nandini had given him was the *gilli* he had first played with. This *gilli* was the reason they were friends—a token of their many adventures and how much they had grown together.

'Nandini, I...' once again, words shied away from him, crawling back into his mind before he could catch them. He felt like a fool—a silly, sentimental fool.

'Yes. I know I gave you the best gift ever. What to do? I am extraordinarily talented.'

David laughed loudly, feeling much less of a fool than before. Nandini realised the worth of the *gilli* in David's life. It was a rewarding feeling to know that there was someone else in the world who looked at things the way she did. It was good to have a friend, who worried about the same little things in life as she did; with whom she could be silly. Someone who truly understood her like no one else did.

~

'David!' his mother called after him, and he grimaced. His mother had not been her usual self for the past few months.

Ever since that evening with Mr Morris, his mother had slowly started denying David of everything he loved about India. Indian food had been forbidden from being served in the household. There was a ban on the use of Hindustani and Indian music. His Indian clothes had probably been burnt, and he was stuck for life with uncomfortable pants and ridiculously thick shirts. In her spree of boycotting all things "Indian," she had also dragged him to her tea parties, forcing him to mingle with children *his age*, as opposed to clinging onto Maya.

'Yes, mother?' he asked her, using every ounce of restraint in his reserve to keep the biting impatience at bay. It was getting increasingly difficult for him to remain composed when she threw a new absurd demand in his direction every time they interacted.

'Where were you?' she barked at him, as if he had committed nothing short of murder by leaving the house.

'I was at ayah*ji*'s house. She threw a surprise party for me.'

'She did *what?*'

Once again, David felt as if his mother was being a tad melodramatic. She made it seem like Maya had to sacrifice a newborn lamb to throw him his surprise party. It was a good thing David was still riding high from the great food and kindness of his friends. Not even his mother's unfair, hysterical whims could dampen his spirits.

'A *surprise* birthday party for me,' David repeated slowly, a goofy smile plastered on his face. It was as if he couldn't fathom the concept himself.

'I see...' his mother nodded curtly, probably unable to find anything to criticise.

'What's that on your forehead?' his mother asked, just when he thought he could slink off.

'Oh, it's a *teeka*. It's a tradition in ayah*ji*'s house. Every family member...'

'You should wash it off,' his mother cut him short.

'Why?' David asked, frowning.

'Because it's...it's...' his mother struggled, wringing her hands together as she tried to come up with an answer.

'Because it looks odd with your attire.'

'On the contrary, I think it complements the white shirt,' David contradicted, feeling like a pretentious snot. It was the only way he could wriggle his way out of his mother's tightening grasp, so it was a price worth paying.

'I do believe, as a woman, I would know more about fashion. And what would people say?' The last part of her sentence came out in a strangled voice, through clenched teeth. It was apparent that she was making an effort to keep calm.

'Since when did you start worrying about what people thought?' David retorted, clearly not worried about keeping his mother's temper in check. He could hardly keep his in check when around her. He couldn't be held responsible for hers.

'David, just wash it off,' his mother repeated more firmly, sighing audibly, almost theatrically.

'But...'

'It would be best if you washed it off,' his mother pressed on, all pretences of remaining calm dropped.

'No, I won't,' he replied, obstinately.

'*David*,' his mother warned, furiously wringing her hands together. David had a feeling she really wanted to strangle him with those very hands at the moment.

'Why is it such a problem?' he asked, trying to keep the frustration out of his voice, and failing.

'You have to consider the effect of your actions on our family before you decide to just go ahead and...'

'How is this *teeka* on my forehead affecting our family, mother?' he asked, glaring at his mother.

'Because, we're not *Indian! For the love of God!* You're *British!*' she shrieked, her hands shaking violently, her face the colour of her favourite red wine.

'So?' he retorted.

'*So?* So, you can't have that ruddy thing on your forehead!' she shouted, running a hand through her already tangled hair.

'But I don't think it would make a difference if I...'

'You're *British*, David. Don't you take *pride* in that?'

'How can I have pride in a country I haven't even been to?' he threw back at his mother, before he could seriously think about what he was saying. He was far too angry to consider the impact of his words. She stared at him blankly with her beady eyes, momentarily stumped.

'David, *that* better not be on your forehead by dinner, or else...' she whispered angrily. There was no mistaking it—she was *threatening* David.

'Or else?' David questioned, barely afraid. He thought he had the right to know why he was being treated like a criminal.

'Or else, I'll lock all your books away.' Had the same *threat* been thrown at David a year ago, he would have panicked and immediately begged her forgiveness. However, no such worries crowded his mind now. He had Nandini by his side, an actual *friend*. He didn't need books for companionship.

'Fine. You can lock them up if you want,' he shrugged, turning his back to his mother and beginning to walk away.

'And you will absolutely not be getting a piece of *your* birthday cake. We had it especially prepared for today.'

'Doesn't matter. I'm quite full with all the food ayah*ji* fed me at her house. *Indian food,*' he said pointedly. He could practically feel his mother's glare, her desperate attempt to issue another *warning*—another way to get him to obey her.

'You should stop seeing that little friend of yours. What was her name? Yes, *Nandini.*' David stopped in his tracks, and turned around, alarmed.

'Nandini?' he asked, gulping and hoping this was a joke.

'Yes, her. It is time you start spending more time with children of *our* kind.'

'Y...you're forbidding me from seeing her?' David stammered, unable to believe this could be happening to him.

'Well, if you put it that way...then, *yes,*' his mother replied, no trace of emotion in her voice.

Yes? YES!

She said it so plainly, without a trace of hesitation or remorse. *Oh,* if only she knew what she was asking him to give up—his dearest companion, one that breathed, laughed, fought and teased him.

His only *real* friend.

~

'David?' Maya opened the door a little, peeking in to find David buried in his covers. He mumbled something incoherent through them, as Maya trotted in.

'Get up, David,' she said softly. Her voice was strained, as if she was trying to hold back something. David got up, expecting to see her smiling face. He was taken aback to find her in a solemn mood. *Were those tears?*

'What's wrong ayah*ji*?' he asked groggily, shifting in his bed to make space for her to sit.

'David...' she sighed loudly, looking at his shoes as she resumed her speech.

'I...I have to leave...' she whispered.

'What! Why?' David cried out, now fully awake.

'Your parents...they...' her voice wavered, she was on the verge of breaking into sobs, so she paused. She took two deep breaths, and started speaking again.

'They thought it would be best if...' she sniffed.

'But...why?' David asked, completely confused.

'They think it is imperative for you to familiarise yourself with your culture. After all, England *is* your home,' Maya couldn't hold back any longer. Over the years, David had become someone she considered as dear to her as Nandini. She saw him as a member of her family, and to let go of him was incredibly painful. As she sobbed silently, David wrapped his arms around her, furiously swallowing the sadness that was threatening to spill in big, fat drops from his eyes.

'I'll still come to meet you at *Chandni Chowk*,' he rubbed her shoulder comfortingly.

'No. You mustn't. Your parents don't want you to.'

'My parents don't want you to stay either. They make *bad* decisions,' David muttered, annoyed.

'No David, you have to respect your parents' wishes. There's a *reason* they're doing all this,' Maya insisted.

'And what would that be?'

'Your parents are under a lot of pressure. They're taking decisions for your own good. They know what's best for you. They're only trying to make sure your future is safe,' Maya insisted, her tone firm. David couldn't understand why she was defending his parents when they had just fired her.

'I understand they are concerned. But that doesn't give them the right to demand you leave all of a sudden without an explanation,' David argued. Maya couldn't help but smile. The David she had first met wouldn't have dared to disagree, let alone criticise his parents. He really had changed, for the better, Maya thought.

'Things have to change, David. You're grown up now, you don't need me.'

'And this thought didn't cross their mind a couple of years ago?' he asked scornfully.

'Perhaps, it did...But things are changing now, David. It can't stay the same forever.'

For some reason, David thought there was something that Maya was hiding from him. Maybe it was the way she was avoiding eye contact, or the way her voice became unnaturally high pitched.

'Are you hiding something from me, ayah*ji*?' he asked.

'N...no...,' she stuttered, her eyes boring into her shoes.

'Ayah*ji*...' David said warningly.

'I think I should leave.'

Maya got up abruptly, and David's eyes widened.

'Wait! You're sure you can't stay?' he asked hopefully, making Maya's heart break. She cupped his face in her hands and planted a kiss on his forehead.

'I have to leave, David. I'm sorry.'

He was finding it very difficult to keep the tears at bay. It physically hurt.

'Don't leave...' he whispered, as she enveloped him into one of her trademark bear hugs.

'I'm sorry, David... it is only for the best...'

She ran her hands through his curly locks, as he retrieved himself from the hug.

'I can't...*not* see you...and *her*...' he said, as tears rolled down his not-so-chubby cheeks.

'I'll tell her about it. She'll understand,' Maya replied. She wiped his tears, slowly, tenderly, as she had done so many times before and started walking away. She paused at the door, and turned to look at David one last time

'Listen to your parents David, but don't change...'

She slammed her fist against her chest, and David nodded, wiping away the flurry of tears.

22

New Delhi, 1943

'Is there something wrong, Mr Wilson?' Ms Jane asked, bemused, as David glared fiercely at the piece of paper he was writing on.

'Uh...no...nothing, Miss,' he looked up at her, and gave a meek smile. It turned out to be more of a grimace.

'Oh, I am sure there's something that's bothering you. What is it?' Ms Jane asked.

Had David not been in a foul mood, he would have returned a warm smile at the concern in her voice. He wasn't aware that his strict, indifferent teacher was capable of being motherly.

'No, I'm fine. Shall we continue with the lesson?' he asked, trying to avoid the topic.

Ms Jane was now *very* concerned. David rarely *ever* wanted to *continue* with his lessons.

'All right, Mr Wilson. Clearly, there's something wrong with you today. Should I call Maya?'

'She's not here,' David replied bitterly.

'Oh, why not? Is it her mother again?'

'No. She was fired,' David muttered, clutching the bottom of the table.

'She was *what?*' Ms Jane questioned, alarmed, not sure she had heard right.

'Fired,' David answered coldly.

'But...why?'

David looked up, rather surprised at his teacher's worry for Maya.

'Because my parents want me to grow up among people of *our* kind and Maya is not one of our *own*,' he replied without any feeling. An image of his old ayah marking his forehead with vermilion popped up in David's mind. She was family to him, more genuine than any of the silly, superficial and uptight people he had met at the tea parties recently. If only his mother understood.

'What a shame. She was quite close to you, wasn't she?' Ms Jane asked. David was quite surprised at the kindness she was showing him. He had been certain that she hated Maya, and all Indian people for that matter.

'Yes. Very,' he answered, trying to push back the waves of heart-wrenching, aching loneliness inside him. He preferred not to think about it much. He wanted to brush aside all the memories that tore him apart every time he revisited them. He buried them in the pages of his books, which he had begun to cling onto again.

'Oh, but what about your other friend? The girl who had come to meet you last year?'

'*Nandini*. You remember her?' David blushed as he blurted her name out, realising only too late that it probably sounded incredibly rude.

'Yes, her. Do you still meet her?' she asked, smiling.

'No.'

He lowered his eyes again, feeling the anger bubbling up from his stomach to his chest. This emotional turmoil had always overpowered him during arguments with his parents. He invariably ended up spurting out something resentful and deeply hurtful. It made him feel awful and ensured a cold silence from his parents for hours afterwards.

'Why? Weren't you very good friends?' Ms Jane asked, frowning. David refrained from rolling his eyes. His teacher's sudden curiosity in his personal life was bordering on aggravating nosiness now.

'Yes. But I told you how my parents want me to fraternise with my *own*. My friendship with Nandini somehow makes me less *patriotic*, at least that's what my mother alleges.'

He spat out the last words venomously, resuming his exercise of glaring at the paper in front of him.

'Oh...' her voice trailed off, and he hoped to God that there were no more questions.

Clearing her throat, Ms Jane started speaking again.

'Would you like to meet her again?' David could discern shyness in her tone as she spoke. He still couldn't come to terms with her sudden gentleness. It was eerie to see her behaving like a human being with *emotions*. Perhaps she'd had a few drinks before their lesson. He idly wondered if he could have a swig or two of whatever she was drinking. He desperately needed it.

'Yes...' he said, shrugging, as if it wasn't that big a deal.

In reality, this was the only thought that preoccupied his mind all the time. Nandini's absence in his life was a constant reminder of his parents' betrayal. There was no point debating this with Ms Jane, she wouldn't be able to do anything anyway. She disliked *Indians*. She was probably in agreement with his parents' decision.

'Well then, I believe I will be able to help you,' she said, and David's head shot up, wincing as he cricked his neck. He gaped at his always stern and austere teacher.

'How?' he almost screeched, much like a banshee. She gave him a stern, hard stare, and he almost sighed in relief. She was still his prim and proper teacher. Things weren't entirely spiralling out of control.

'Well, this is only if you *really* want to meet her.'

'Yes...' David urged her to continue, impatient.

'You can leave for the first-half of our lessons. Your mother barely ever checks in, and if she ever does, I'll say I've sent you to my house to fetch a book. My house is down the road,' she explained the plan.

David slumped in his chair, shaking his head.

'It won't work. There's no *way* she'll buy that.'

'Oh, believe me, she *will*. She trusts me. She would never suspect me,' her eyes sparkled with the excitement that was gushing out in her words.

David couldn't help but wonder whether she had ever been a *rebel* in her life. He, for one, would never have pegged her as one, considering her stiff appearance. Not a hair was ever out of place.

'But you *must* return in time, so we can do some work,' she resumed with the formality she usually wrapped around herself, like a protective cloak.

'Yes, miss. All right,' he said, nodding.

He figured he might as well give her idea a shot. It was better than nothing.

'Well! Are you just going to sit here or get up and go meet your friend?'

'Oh, right!' David got up, smiling gratefully at his teacher. 'Thank you.'

'You're welcome. Now go! You may have the *full lesson* for today. But *only* today.'

He nodded and he reached for the French window near his study table. His hand hovered over the lever, but curiosity got the better of him.

'But, why are you helping me?' David asked.

'Because I lost my chance at love. I don't want you to go through the same,' she smiled at him, and he shook his head violently.

'She's not...I'm not in love with her,' he said, horrified by the mere thought of it. Nandini, was, and would always be a friend—a best friend. Nothing other than that.

'Yes, but you do *love* her?' asked his teacher, amused by his horror.

'Yes, like a best friend,' David replied, smiling.

'Well then, go and meet her.'

'Right,' he repeated, feeling incredibly idiotic. He jumped out of his seat, and yanked open the window. He was so excited; he almost didn't notice his beloved *Jungle Book* figurine smashing to pieces on the floor. He glanced momentarily at it, before propping his leg above the ledge, bracing himself to jump.

'Aren't you going to fix that?' his teacher asked, a few seconds before he was about to jump.

'No, it's not important,' he replied, his hand digging into his pocket, his fingers running over rough, splintered wood. Finally, he jumped off the windowsill and ran out of the bungalow with a huge smile plastered on his face.

~

'Nandini!'

Nandini turned around, her face breaking into a delightful smile as David skipped up to her.

'David!' she exclaimed, wrapping her arms around his neck.

'Hello!' he whispered happily, returning the hug.

'How? I thought you were...' Nandini retrieved herself from the hug, visibly baffled.

'I was...I mean I am. But my teacher helped me.'

'What? The one who you always said *hates Indians*?' Nandini asked, astonished.

'Yes, apparently she doesn't,' he responded, grinning.

'That's great! Jalebis?'

'Definitely.'

23

New Delhi, 1944

David and Nandini's rendezvous became a weekly event. Since Chandni Chowk and Lodhi Colony were far from each other, the two friends chose to meet at a central place in the city. It proved to be easier for Nandini as well, who was still fighting with her father and couldn't afford to be seen with David. Her father would certainly become even more upset if he found out. David's secret meetings with Nandini helped him deal with his parents at home. It was an act of silent rebellion, which, under the tyranny of his parents, was a source of comfort.

David met Maya a few times, but she was not quite approving of his *discrete* ways of meeting Nandini. At first, she was furious with him for defying his parents, but later when he had reasoned with her, she stopped glaring at him and throwing him dirty looks.

His mother was misled into believing that the new improvement in his son's character was a result of his effort to spend more time mingling with *people his own kind* and his teacher, Ms Jane. While David had started growing a *grudging* respect for his teacher, he still couldn't say he liked her. That is of course, until she told him her tragic love story. He was blown away by how fearless and honest she was. Had it been anyone else, David thought, they would have been too shy or ashamed to talk about their private life.

Ms Jane, however, was neither.

'Sorry I'm late, got a bit caught up,' David greeted his teacher, jumping in through the French windows leading to his room. His teacher looked up from her book, waving off his apology.

'It is not a problem. Try coming back early from next week.'

They began the lessons. From tackling complex arithmetic questions, the student and the teacher gradually progressed to the nuances of grammar and language. David was soon bored out of his mind, and his thoughts started wandering.

For David, it was quite intriguing to imagine his ever serious and seemingly dull tutor in love with somebody. He cleared his throat, mustering the courage to finally pose the question that had been bothering him for a long time now, today.

'So...erm...why are you helping?' He scrunched up his face, remembering he had asked her that question before.

'I thought we discussed this already, Mr Wilson,' she replied, not looking up from the book in front of her. Obviously they had discussed it before, but she hadn't given the...details of her story.

'Yes, but...what...what happened exactly...?' David's voice trailed off, his cheeks flushed as her head shot up and her narrowing eyes scrutinised his face.

'Are you trying to ask me what happened with me?'

'Well...no...yes...' David mumbled, running his fingers across one edge of the table.

He felt extremely foolish.

'Right...well...' she faltered, possibly trying to decide where to begin the story.

'I was tutoring a child, much like you, in Amritsar.'

'Was he British?'

'Yes. He had a manservant looking after him. His name was Baldev. I was *very* young.'

Suddenly, David understood. *Of course!* It all made sense now. Why she felt uncomfortable around Indian people. Why she was so stiff and grey. She had been broken. She had lost someone she wanted to spend the rest of her life with, and had been told that she had been wrong in loving him. Every Indian person was a constant reminder of what she had lost. She didn't hate them; she just couldn't be reminded of something that had probably altered the shape of her being. He wouldn't want to either, if he were in her position.

'How old were you?' David's cheeks immediately flushed as he posed this question. He had been taught very early on in his life that it was terribly rude to ask a lady her age. Ms Jane's lip curled into a smirk. Evidently, *she* didn't seem to mind being asked about her age, current or not.

'Twenty', she replied.

'Well, we fell in love, but our employers found out. And... he got fired.'

'Did you get fired?' Ms Jane shook her head, and he frowned.

'No, the boy was fond of me, and there weren't many qualified tutors around at the time.'

'I...see...'

'Yes, and we couldn't really see each other for a while. He'd been told that he would be...dismembered if he ever came near me.'

'He'd be...dismembered?' David asked, not sure whether he had heard right. Surely, you couldn't be punished so severely for falling in *love!*

'Yes. He had been threatened that his hands would be cut off or something equally ridiculous.' She elaborated quite casually, unmoved. David appeared visibly shocked at his teacher's nonchalance.

'But we decided we'd run away. Elope. We'd set the date a day after the Jallianwala Bagh massacre,' she took a deep breath, curling the end of a piece of paper lying on the desk in front of her.

'He...he...he was in the Jallianwala Bagh when...' she broke off, turning her head away from David. He could see a tear trickle down her face. He nearly placed his hand on her shoulder, but withdrew just in time. She wasn't the sort of person who wanted to be comforted. She would take it as pity, David was sure of it.

'I...' he wavered, grasping for words that could be of any solace to her. *Sorry* did not seem to be a word big enough to console her. How could an *apology* suffice for a woman who lost her love, a day before she was to start a new life with him?

The reality of the massacre—something he had considered as horrifying, yes, but a figment of history, suddenly hit him with greater intensity. He hadn't really considered what the repercussions of Jallianwala Bagh, or other atrocities would be for the families, the friends involved with those who died.

They sat there, uneasy in each other's company, unable to break the tension that has settled in the air. The silence was miserable. It bred thoughts and worries, especially for David, who now regretted having urged Ms Jane to share her story.

His austere teacher was quietly reminiscing. There was something about immersing oneself in nostalgia—it was hauntingly beautiful and empty, yet therapeutic at the same time. Had she been asked to narrate the story five years ago, she would have collapsed in no time. Now, however, she had learnt the art of holding herself together. She had come to terms with her reality.

The door to David's room burst open and he thanked God for this unexpected intrusion.

'David!' his hysterical mother barged into the room. David was certain his mother was on the threshold of senility.

'Mother...' he said apprehensively, dreading the next crazy demand that she would impose on him.

'I need to talk to you,' she said, leaning against the door for support. Something told David that she had one too many glasses of wine.

'Erm...all right then...' he looked at her expectantly, waiting for her to begin ranting about something trivial and irrelevant.

'*Alone*,' she said, pointedly glaring at Ms Jane. Bowing her head, his teacher walked out. After Ms Jane's exit, David's mother staggered to his desk and sat on the chair that had previously been occupied by the teacher.

'What is it, mother?' David asked, genuinely concerned. She was never rude to Ms Jane. She looked like a complete mess with her mascara trickling down her cheeks, leaving an ugly trail behind.

'I want you to answer my question truthfully,' she said, holding his hands and staring squarely at him. David's concern grew, if possible, larger, pumping fiercely in his chest. Somehow, he managed to nod his head, fighting the stress that was slamming against his ribcage.

'Do you have *any* information about any members of the Congress?'

All colour evaporated from David's face, his hands suddenly turned cold. He gaped at her, blinking several times, looking like an idiot. He felt his heart beat faster. The stress turned into full-fledged panic, banging against his insides, demanding to be let out in loud, ugly screams. Why was his mother asking him about the Congress members? How could she know about Nandini and her father?

'W...why?' David stammered, trying very hard not to start shaking like a petrified little dog. He wasn't sure he'd be able to lie convincingly to his mother, her eyes drilling into him.

'Because if you do, it would be incredibly helpful,' she squeezed his hands, in an attempt to comfort him, smiling. Her smile sent shivers down his spine.

David was positive something was *very* wrong.

'What's wrong, mother?' he asked, worried.

'Oh...nothing...' she casually waved off his concern, completely unconvincing.

'What's wrong, mother?' he repeated the question, firmly.

'David, if you could please help me without interrogating too much then...'

'Why?' David interrupted, now affronted.

'Listen David, if there's *anything* that you know, *please,* do not hide.'

'Mother, even if I *did* know anything, I wouldn't tell you. It is a matter of confidentiality.'

'No! You *must* tell me! You don't understand David, it is imperative to...'

'*You* don't understand, mother. I can't betray other people's trust just to keep pace with your unprecedented interest in politics.'

'David! I am your *mother*, for the love of *God*, just *listen* to me. Can't you trust *me*?'

'Of course I trust you, but that doesn't mean I'm going to betray someone who trusts me. I cannot let them down.' David explained, trying to pacify his frantic mother.

'David, please, *please*,' his mother pleaded, grabbing his hands again, her eyes brimming with tears.

David wrapped his arms around his mother's shaking shoulders, cradling her head. In an instant their roles were reversed.

How could his ever elegant, calm and composed mother become such a mess? Why had she completely broken down like this?

'What's wrong, mother?' David whispered in her ears. Sniffling, her mother lifted her head from his chest. David noticed the dark circles under her eyes. She hadn't slept well for days. Now, these frequent bouts of hysteria were making sense.

'David...your father's in jail. You know how we embraced Indian culture. We bought Indian clothes, served Indian food at our parties and even spoke Hindustani at home. There was resentment brewing against our way of living and how we continued throwing lavish parties even during wartime. All that silly wine I ordered... And someone saw you helping that Indian man during the protest march. Every action of ours was interpreted pro-Indian and anti-British.'

David went numb. Guilt flooded him, coursing through his body as viscous, sluggish blood. How could he have been so oblivious to the changes around him? How had the tension that now seemed to have tightened its grip around his family completely escaped him the past few weeks? Had he really been so self-absorbed? Had he really been so distant from his parents? His father was an important army officer. The arrest couldn't just have *happened!* There was clearly much more to his mother's hysteria and borderline alcoholism that David had unfortunately ignored or perhaps misinterpreted as early signs of senility. Looking at his mother's predicament—her degeneration from being a woman with high self-esteem to a helpless wife worried about her husband's release—David promised himself that he would be a more responsible son. He was determined to make things better.

24

New Delhi, 1944

'What! That's ridiculous! They can't do that!' David exclaimed, outraged.

'They're the government, David. They run the country. They can do whatever they want,' his mother replied, sighing. The thought was not a happy one, but David knew that his mother wasn't half wrong.

After overcoming the initial shock of the news of his father's imprisonment, David demanded an explanation from his mother. None of the 'you're-still-a-child' nonsense would do.

Apparently, the Wilsons were infamous for their excessive benevolence toward *Indians*. David helping an old, injured man during the protest march and Mr Wilson not shying away from inviting Indian guests to his parties were a few episodes that earned this family a bad reputation in the neighbourhood. What landed David's father in jail was his role in ensuring that members of the INA and Congress leaders could protest in peace. That, for the government, was the last straw.

It seemed ridiculous to David that his father had been imprisoned for doing his job. David's mother explained that the government claimed his father was an accomplice of the protestors, giving them classified information.

'Your father's release depends on our decision. If we provide the names of the members of the INA and give details about other Congress leaders to the government, then we can definitely free him. Those underground members...'

'I...I don't know if...' David sighed, frustrated. He didn't know which way to go.

'I won't pressurise you, you can take your time to arrive at a decision,' his mother cupped his face and planted a kiss on his forehead. David was immediately reminded of Maya.

Innumerable confusing thoughts buzzed in his head. He honestly did not know what to do. Should he choose family over his friends? Should his allegiance to his family and the British overrule bonds of friendship with Nandini, Maya and others?

David weighed his choices and found himself torn between the love for his family and the love for the friends amongst whom he had found another family.

How could he abandon his parents? His life was a gift from his father and mother. They were the reason Maya had walked into his life. Maya was the one who brought Nandini into his life. He knew that he could make mistakes and destroy every other relationship in the world, but the one that he had with his parents would remain forever. His parents would forgive all his mistakes. Then...shouldn't he betray Nandini's trust for their sake? Should he stand by his parents at all cost?

He dug his hand in his pocket, his fingers running over the rough surface of the chipped, wooden *gilli*—the *gilli* that Nandini had given him on his birthday last year.

He had pledged never to break her trust. But now, and by revealing the secrets that she had requested him to guard with his life, he would inevitably have to break that promise, break her trust; probably, put an end to their friendship.

He remembered Maya telling him to not *change*. She had told him that he should listen to his parents, but not at the risk of compromising with his own character. Maya...the person who had brought a hurricane of change—of colour, conflict, courage and such great joy; how would he bring himself to break her unwavering faith in him?

He remembered his mother's heart-wrenching sobs and dishevelled appearance. His mother—who had given birth to him, who had tried her best to give him a secure life—lay devastated, agonising and crestfallen.

The memories of his father crowded David's mind. His booming laughter, his peculiar way of twisting his moustache while narrating stories, haunted David. He remembered how his father would always put his arm around David's shoulder, and introduce him to guests with much pride.

He couldn't imagine what his father must be going through in prison. The man who had taught him to read, ride a bicycle and fish was now languishing behind bars. He had always seemed so strong and unbreakable. David didn't want to think about what they were doing to him, how they were breaking his seemingly indestructible father.

He shuddered. What was he to do?

25

New Delhi, Sharma Household, 1944

It was a typical family dinner in the Sharma household. After days, things began going back to being normal and pleasant. Nandini and her father, although did not reconcile, decided to forget about their feud and move on. Her father looked a lot more relaxed than he usually did.

'Babuji, do you think we'll get rid of the British very soon?' Nandini asked.

'Yes, I do. I think the war has already started taking a toll on Britain. They won't really have a choice but to give India up.'

'Yes, I was reading something that Nehruji had written...'

'*Of course* you were,' her father teased, his eyes twinkling mischievously. Nandini grinned, not particularly fazed by her father's jab at her overt fascination with Nehru. It meant things were going back to normal.

Nandini was about to retort, but was interrupted by the doorbell.

Sighing loudly, her father got up and walked over to the main door.

'Are you Vikas Sharma?' a gruff voice enquired, in broken Hindustani. Nandini frowned, confused. Why was there a British person visiting their house at this hour of the night? As far as she knew, she was the only one in the family with a British friend, and he was too scared of her father to turn up at her doorstep unwarranted.

'Yes...' her father answered.

'I'm afraid you'll have to come with me.' Nandini heard the clicking of metal, and craned her neck to see what was going on.

'Why?' her father asked, calmly.

'Because you are under arrest.'

Nandini shot up and ran up to her father.

'What's happening?' Nandini asked the officer, who in turn ignored her presence.

'On what charges officer?' Nandini's father asked.

Nandini was amazed at her father's composure. He was literally being dragged to jail and he still managed to remain calm, as if he was simply being invited for dinner at the police station.

'We have a witness who claimed that you were one of the participants in the recent bridge burnings, protests and demonstrations against the government.'

'All right, let's go then,' Vikas extended his wrists, smiling, unperturbed, at the police officer. The officer clasped handcuffs around Nandini's father's bony wrists. Unlike her father, Nandini was a failure when it came to observing rules of serenity.

'No! Babuji, they don't have enough proof!' Nandini grabbed onto her father's arm, desperately trying to pull him back. She wanted to throw up her half-eaten dinner and wrap herself around her father's leg like she used to as a child.

'We have a very reliable witness, *Miss*,' the police officer spat out the last word spitefully.

'Who?' Nandini screeched, tightening her grip on her father's arm, refusing to let go. Tears threatened to spill over from her eyes, but the policeman remained unmoved.

'That is confidential information, but I assure you that he is very reliable.'

'But...'

'Nandu, don't worry. It won't be long, I'll be back soon.'

'Nandu, let go,' her mother pulled her away from her father.

'NO! Babuji!' Nandini's heart sank as she watched her father being taken away, handcuffed.

Vikas Sharma didn't look back and walked out with his head held high.

'He'll be back very soon, Nandu. Don't worry, let's go inside,' her mother tried to put on a brave face in front of her daughter.

As she turned around, Nandini couldn't believe her eyes at what she saw next.

Nikhil trudged up to the police officer standing next to him, head bent. He was handcuffed as well.

It wasn't until her father and Nikhil had been shoved into the police van that the officer's words sunk in, and like poison, chilled her bones with horror.

He is very reliable...

As far as Nandini knew, there was only one other person apart from Nikhil who knew that her father was organising demonstrations against the government. Something cold and slippery slid down her throat, her mouth felt dry.

'Nandu. I told you to come inside, where are you going?' her mother barked after her daughter.

'I'm not going after babuji, Ma,' Nandini replied.

'Then, where exactly are you headed at this time?' her grandmother intervened.

'To find some answers.'

She hoped her dramatic, mysterious reply, would satisfy both her nagging mother and grandmother. Unfortunately, her grandmother was not in a forgiving mood. Not only had her son been imprisoned, her rebellious, *unladylike* granddaughter was now proposing to venture out at an ungodly hour. What would people say?

'Find your answers tomorrow.'

Nandini was determined.

'Dadi*ji*, I'll come back soon. It's absolutely urgent that I go see this person.'

'What did you say?'

Her grandmother's glare was menacing as ever. Nandini was almost certain she would start breathing fire through her nose soon.

'Dadi...I really...'

'No. You don't. I've had enough of your running around, talking to boys, and *defaming* our family. As it is, your father is determined to do dangerous, silly things. I will not allow you to follow in his footsteps.'

Defaming our family?

What was so wrong about talking to and playing with boys? Then, it struck her. Her grandmother was worried about her! She wanted Nandini to be safe. As touched as she was though, her grandmother's surprising show of concern for her wasn't going to stop her.

'But dadi...'

'Vikas is not here right now, so you have to listen to me. Don't even try to beg, I'm not Vikas. I won't relent.'

What could she say after that? She knew her grandmother was being unreasonable, but she was helpless.

As much as she'd wanted to go punch the living daylights out of David Wilson, she couldn't disobey her grandmother. It would mean a world of pain for her mother, who had enough to deal with already.

'It's your fault that my son's in jail today. If you weren't with that *firang* all the time...'

Nandini's grandmother hobbled away, presumably cursing Nandini and her *firang* friend under her breath. Nandini couldn't help but smile. At least her grandmother was behaving like her normal, taunting, infuriating self.

'Nandu...don't mind her. I know it wasn't your fault.'

Nandini's mother was the only rational being in this situation of crisis. She did not blame anybody. She comforted her daughter and reaffirmed that everything was going to be just *fine*. Not this time though. For Nandini, the problem was far too grave to be solved by a warm hug.

'How do you know it will be fine, Ma?' For a while, her mother didn't say anything, and Nandini was sure that, this time, she didn't have an answer to her question.

'Because I'm going to join the fight now. And I mean it. I will not let your father's dream of carrying forward the Party's objectives and goals be aborted too soon. I also promise to have him back with us very soon. I know he will be.'

'But what about dadi*ji*?'

'Don't worry about that. Everything will be fine soon.'

~

Wrapped in her mother's protective arms, Nandini felt the sickening taste of guilt, sticking to the roof of her mouth, insurmountable. She could sense a huge battle brewing between her mother and her grandmother. Her father was in jail. Her mother was going to have to run around fulfilling all household duties and step into the shoes of her father, at the same time, ensuring the Party didn't fall apart in the wake of his sudden arrest. Life had been made more difficult now.

If only she hadn't been with that firang all the time…

~

'Nandu…are you all right?' Maya asked, placing a warm, comforting hand on her teenage neighbour's shoulder. Nandini Sharma flinched. 'Di…What are you doing here?' she mumbled groggily, staring at Maya as if she was seeing her after years.

'I came to check on you. I…I was worried.'

Nandini's silence and her red-rimmed puffy eyes made Maya anxious.

Nandini Sharma barely ever got speechless. She had an inexhaustible supply of energy, and countless thoughts that she was constantly compelled to voice.

Nandini had lost both—her voice, and her thoughts.

Images of her father, handcuffed, flashed through her mind every now and then. She felt an invisible rope tighten around her chest, threatening to snap her ribcage.

It hurt so much.

'Yes…I'm all right.'

'I really am…' Nandini insisted, the rope almost strangulating her now.

Both Maya and Nandini looked miserable.

'I just don't understand how this could happen?' Maya spoke, breaking the silence.

Nandini felt sick in her stomach. Guilt flooded every pore of her body, as she remembered those conversations, where he promised to *never* tell anyone.

'Di...'

She gulped, trying to swallow the bitter pill of regret and remorse. Maya stared expectantly at her. Nandini took a deep breath, and motivated herself to let out the truth.

'It was *me*...' she mumbled.

Maya frowned, confused.

'What was?'

'I told David about...about the...' she faltered, struggling to continue. How could she? She had been so *stupid!* And now the most important person in her life was imprisoned.

'*He* told the authorities?'

All Nandini could do was nod.

'That...' Maya paused, biting her tongue before something incredibly spiteful came out of her mouth.

'I trusted him, and he's the reason...' Nandini's voice broke off, as she buried her head in her arms, muffling her cries. Maya sighed, and silently stroked Nandini's head.

'Nandu...you don't worry. I'm going to go and...'

Nandini's head shot up, and she shook her head violently.

'No! Don't!' Nandini shouted, startling Maya. Maya raised her hands in the air, as if in surrender.

'All right. I won't. But, why?' she asked calmly, hoping her tone would soothe the harried Nandini.

'Because...he doesn't deserve our time. You think I wouldn't have gone there, first thing?'

'Yes, I was wondering. Why didn't you go to him?'

'Dadiji didn't let me. And then I calmed down, and I realised that I don't want anything from him.'

'You came to this conclusion *after* you calmed down?' Nandini nodded, turning a blind eye to Maya's raised eyebrows.

'And I decided that if I didn't have anything to say to him, then why should I go and see him? Wouldn't that be a waste of time?'

Maya smiled, marvelling at how mature little Nandini had become. It seemed like only yesterday, when she was running around the streets of Chandni Chowk, creating havoc with her gang of friends.

Perhaps, it had only been yesterday.

'Well, if you want to do that, you can. But I am going to go and pay David Wilson a visit.'

'But didi...'

'I'll see you later, Nandu.'

Before Nandini could even open her mouth to reply, Maya had gone. Nandini groaned, her head slumping on the table once again.

There were a few ways this could go. *None of them could be good.*

~

'DAVID! DAVID WILSON!'

David peered out of the double doors into the garden as he heard his name being screamed. For a moment he had thought it was Nandini.

'David, I believe someone is calling for you outside,' David's mother said, smiling brightly at her son. Ever since David had taken the *decision*, her mood had improved considerably.

'Oh, all right. I'll go outside.'

He saw Maya standing outside on the road, glowering at him. Never before had he seen such *malice* in his soft-spoken ayah*ji*'s eyes.

'Ayah*ji* what are you...'

'Don't call me that. How long did you think you could hide in your palace?' she practically spat at him, her words drenched in venomous hatred.

It hit David suddenly. *She must have found out*. The guilt that he had kept locked in a corner of his mind assaulted his senses. He could feel a thousand tiny needles pricking at his insides. There were so many things he wanted to say, but he didn't have the courage to say any of them. He had done something he knew was unforgivable.

'I...I don't know...'

'Don't you *dare* play dumb'

David blinked dumbly at Maya. She was right. He shouldn't pretend like it didn't happen, like he didn't know what he had done. That was worse than the actual act of betrayal that he had so helplessly committed.

'I...' His thoughts bounced around his head. None of them were turning into concrete words.

'She *trusted* you!' Maya exclaimed, her eyes tearing up. He hated that word. *Trust*. It was tossed around as if it were a plastic ball from a beachside resort—cheap, easily available, and temporary. He couldn't handle the weight of the word. The true meaning of it. He was selfish and weak. He crumbled like shortbread in times of distress.

'I...' He repeated dully.

'Is that all you have to say for yourself?' Maya demanded, partially curious. Perhaps he had a good explanation for his stupidity.

'I had to do it. My...' the words fell out of his mouth automatically. He felt like someone else had said them. It didn't sound like him—to offer excuses for his unforgivable crime.

'My brother's in jail. Nandini's father is in jail. Your best friend hasn't slept for two days and you have the audacity to say that you had to do it?'

Everything seemed to freeze for a moment. There was complete silence, as David processed the words. *Jail. Just like his father.*

'He's in...w...what?' David fumbled, completely in shock. He had not known that his tattling could lead to Nandini's father going to jail! And Nikhil... He had been nothing but kind to David. He could taste rusting iron, stuck to the roof of his mouth. It was the guilt that he had pushed to the back of his mind.

'I'm so sorry...I didn't know this was going to...'

'Oh yes, of *course* you didn't, because when you give names of freedom fighters, the *last* thing you would expect is for them to get *arrested*.'

'I'm really sorry, ayah*ji*. What else can I say? I had to—I had to do what I did. Nandini taught me to do what I believed in and I did that.'

David had been promised that no one was going to be imprisoned. Perhaps it had been naïve of him to believe it, but he never *meant* for things to take a disastrous turn. He wasn't sure his ayahji would be impressed with his intentions.

'You don't get it, do you? They went to jail because of *you*. I treated you like a member of our family. I gave you more love than I thought possible. I...' she faltered, swallowing the lump that had begun to form in her throat. Her inability to speak didn't stop her from glaring at David, as if he were a parasite that was infecting everything around him. It wasn't far from what he felt like—a disgusting, toxic sycophant who sucked every bit of his friends' happiness. Never in the five years that she had been with him had David given Maya a reason to be upset. He couldn't bear to think of what Nandini was going through. He remembered how miserable she had been when fighting with her father. He was her entire world. She almost worshipped him, and to see him getting dragged away in shackles must have destroyed her completely.

'What is all this?' David was somewhat relieved that his mother had come to distract him from his searing remorse and shame. Then, he saw the frosty, almost lethal looks exchanged between his mother and Maya. It made him want to put as much distance between the two women as possible.

'Nothing, mother. You can go inside,' David muttered quietly, hoping that his mother would not create a scene.

'Absolutely not, David. Rishi, tell this woman to leave immediately,' she turned to the guard, who stared blankly at her. David buried his face in his hands, now absolutely certain that things were going to get much, much worse.

'I'm sorry Memsahib, but I can't do that. She's outside, on the road, and I can only throw people out of your property. The street is not your property.'

David's mother scoffed, offended, at the guard, who shrugged nonchalantly. David mentally cursed the guard. Surely he could have chosen a better time to show solidarity with Maya. There was only one thing David could do now. He walked up to the gate, opening it himself and staring stonily at his mother. He didn't like being so harsh with her, especially after his father's imprisonment. She had become so jumpy, so terrified of the slightest sound. She picked up every letter they received with trembling hands, as if it had been dipped in poison.

'Mother, will you please go inside?' David asked her firmly, his tone stern. She stared at him blankly for a second, taken aback. Somehow, he managed to retain his composure, and defeated, his mother walked inside the house without another word. Heaving a sigh of relief, David turned to Maya, who was still glaring at him with unadulterated revulsion.

'Ayah*ji*, if you'll just let me explain...'

'I don't want an explanation,' Maya said coldly.

'But if you just *listen*...'

'No David, I don't want to listen to you.'

'Just for a moment...'

'No, why don't you understand...'

'JUST LISTEN TO ME FOR TWO MINUTES!' David shouted, shocking both Maya and himself. He had never shouted at anyone, let alone the woman he respected the most. Rishi, the guard retained the blank expression on his face, and stood rooted to the spot. He probably shouldn't have shouted, but she *had* to understand. He *had* to explain to her. She couldn't stay upset with him like that. It wasn't right!

'My father was in jail. We were told that they would set him free if we gave them details of the members of the Congress or INA to the government.'

'So in order to free your father, you sold out on your promise?'

'I had no choice! You don't know what it was like at home these past few weeks. I couldn't let him rot in jail!' David exclaimed despairingly.

'There's always a choice David. You just chose selfishly,' Maya murmured, turning away from him and walking off. It felt like her words had slashed at his skin. David hadn't ever felt such immense, intense pain before.

'Ayah*ji*, wait!'

David ran up to her. She couldn't just leave! Not without forgiving him.

'I'd told you. Listen to your parents, but don't change who you are,' she stabbed where it hurt the most.

'I...I had...'

Maya didn't wait for David to finish. Without even a glance at him, she stalked away. The meek apology, that David tried to mumble, died on his lips. His last words to his beloved ayah*ji* were lost in the swirl of dust that she left behind.

~

Nandini could barely remember the last time she had felt so utterly euphoric. None of Pandit*ji*'s speeches or writings had made her feel this ecstatic. The sight of her father and Nikhil bhaiya, returning from prison, made her want to scream from the rooftops. When her father wrapped his arms around her, all Nandini could do was cry like a stupid child. She buried her head in his old clothes and wept uncontrollably. Vikas tried to shush her, but miraculously his affectionate act made her feel overwhelmingly sentimental. He wasn't ready to let go of his little girl. Not after the torture he had endured the past few weeks. He was almost certain he was dreaming, but maybe if he held Nandini tight enough, it might turn out to be true.

'It's all right Nandu. I'm right here,' his voice cracked toward the end, and Nandini had a strong suspicion that he was crying as well.

Somehow, Nandini managed to stop her pathetic snivelling, and detached herself from her father.

She looked up at him and saw him offer her a wobbly smile. Wiping her nose, Nandini laced her fingers with her father's and led him to the chair that he normally occupied.

'You don't look terrible,' Nandini remarked, inspecting her father. Nikhil gasped, shocked at Nandini's audacity to talk to her father that way. To him, Vikas was a perfect vision of the battered hero. Not that he would ever tell Vikas that. He was far too scared.

Vikas laughed loudly, the corners of his eyes crinkling. Nandini was relieved to see him returning to his normal self. He had seemed almost terrified when he first entered the house.

'Thank you my dear. I was worried I had lost my sense of style in jail,' he teased her.

'No, I mean you don't seem...it seems like they didn't beat you black and blue.'

'Yes, well, Nikhil took most of it. He was quite the *hero*,' Vikas smiled at Nikhil, and Nandini could almost see her neighbour's chest puff up with pride.

'That is not true. Vikas*ji* was beaten thrice by the police officers.'

'He was *what?*'

Nandini winced, as Vikas glared at Nikhil for his lack of tact. Nikhil's chest immediately deflated, and his gaze dropped to the ground, ashamed.

'Nothing darling, Nikhil is just being modest,' Vikas answered his daughter's question a tad too nonchalantly. His wife scoffed, as she thrust the cup of tea in his hand.

'I...I should go. Maya and Ma will be really excited to see me.' Nikhil muttered quietly, hardly waiting for a response before scampering away.

'Wait, bhaiya! I wanted to see Maya didi too,' Nandini ran after Nikhil, leaving her parents alone.

'Always trying to be a *hero*,' Shantala muttered, scowling darkly at her husband. Vikas smiled and tenderly reached out for her hand.

'I've heard you were quite stupendous in my absence. Come, have your tea,' he wrapped his arms around her shoulder, as she complied and sat next to him. He lifted the cup, and she took a sip.

'You went to all my meetings? And all our rallies.'

'I did.'

'Ma was fine with all of that?'

'She was very upset at first. But as long as I was home to make dinner, she wasn't too bothered. Nandini was very helpful.'

'Yes, I was wrong about her. She really has grown up in the past few years.' Shantala smiled, and reached for her husband's empty cup and saucer. Vikas cleared his throat, as if he had something urgent to say.

'I was also wrong about...you. I'm...I'm very sorry. I didn't even consider what you wanted to do in our fight for independence. I thought you were happy...'

'Don't apologise. I never told you. But now that you know...' Shantala lingered on the last syllable hopefully, waiting for her husband to say something, praying he would support her. It had been easy to pretend that he wanted her to take over his responsibilities when he hadn't been there. She wasn't sure that was what he actually wanted.

'And now that I know, I'm going to make sure that I never stop you or get in your way. I'll have Nandini scream at me if I ever do,' Shantala chuckled.

'We were so worried. Maa*ji* only ate once a day,' Nandini's mother said, after a short silence.

'And how many times did you eat?'

'Oh, I ate all three meals. I wasn't worried at all.' Vikas snorted at his wife's poor attempt at concealing the truth. She teased him for being the martyr, but she was quite the tragic heroine herself.

'I missed your chai. The sugarless chai at the police station was horrible.'

'Well, maybe I should teach them how to make a proper cup of tea for your next stay there,' she let out a giggle as Vikas feigned being offended, spluttering dramatically.

It was good to be home.

26

London, 2011

'And I never saw her again.'

My granddad concluded the story.

I stared, open-mouthed at him, unable to digest the words he had just spoken.

I couldn't believe that my *own* granddad, whom I dearly loved and believed was the epitome of goodness and morality, had *betrayed* his friend. I had always looked up to him. I couldn't fathom him *ever* doing something so disastrous. How could he destroy someone's life? How could he sell his friendship, even if it was for his father's sake?

'I can't believe you did that!' It came out before I could control myself—the accusation and the disgust.

'W...what?' he was taken aback. Why wouldn't he be? I had never been so disrespectful. I had never seen him as weak or wrong or *small*. I couldn't get it through my head. He *had* been wrong. He had been immeasurably cruel and selfish. All my life he had taught me to follow my heart; he had me convinced that there is nothing more important than kindness and selflessness. And he had managed to destroy everything he stood for, everything I stood for in a single narrative.

'She was your best-friend, and you pawned away your friendship.' The words got caught in my throat as I forced them out. It was hard for me to believe that I was talking to him like that. It was hard to think that he deserved it.

There was a silence, which drew for far longer than either of us cared for. He sighed loudly and looked so old all of a sudden. He'd shrunk again. His hunched back and his papery, wrinkling skin stretched over his face, fitting poorly. It made me pity him. Pity how small he looked, and how his eyes were drenched in self-loathing and regret.

'I know, and I was really ashamed...'

'That didn't stop you from doing the wrong thing, did it?' I demanded from him, bitterly. I didn't feel bad enough for him to forgive what he had done. There wasn't much I could think about. My mind was flooded with rage and betrayal. He had betrayed me. He had *lied* to me. He had projected this image of perfection. I had put him on a pedestal, and he ended up being horrifyingly human. It was painful to see him topple off the pedestal I had put him on.

'I don't understand how...'

'I can't believe you, granddad. You had me convinced...' I spat out, my eyes glinting maliciously. I didn't have much control over what I was saying. Words rushed out in a flurry, without asking me for permission.

'Emily, I'm not sure where...'

'Forget it, granddad. I'm leaving,' I rose from my seat, and grabbing my jacket and school bag, stomped out of the room. I had never felt so regretful and disgusted at the same time.

How could he?

~

27

Ranchi, 2011

'So, what happened after?' I asked my grandma, my feet dangling off the sofa that I had sprawled on.

We were in my grandma's living room. It was the last week of my holidays and I was incredibly sorry to go. The more time I spent with my grandma, the more reluctant I was to go back to the city I had been yearning for a few weeks ago.

'Well, babu*ji* got bail in two weeks' time; soon after Maya didi gave David her piece of mind.'

'Really? How come?' I asked, surprised.

'Because David got him bail,' she said, smiling.

'How do you know?'

My grandma just smiled mysteriously, and shrugged, as if it wasn't something to ponder over.

'I just did...' she answered, almost smirking as I gaped at her. *She couldn't leave me hanging like that, could she?* Undoubtedly, she knew that *not* knowing would torture me. This little, undisclosed detail would keep me awake at night. I was as invested in her story as she was in her soap operas.

'Seriously naani, how did you know?' I asked, trying to keep my voice level, so as not to betray my frustration. She laughed loudly, but started coughing in between. Worried, I got up and quickly poured her a glass of water.

'Here,' I said, handing it to her and rubbing her back.

'Thank you.'

'And what happened after the war ended? It ended in '45, didn't it?' she nodded, surprised, once again, by my knowledge of history.

'I *know* history, I just don't like it much,' I confessed, shrugging nonchalantly.

'If you insist,' she said as I glared at her, and I couldn't help but break into a smile.

'So when did you leave Delhi?'

'Much later babu*ji* decided to move to Benaras.'

'Why?'

'Babu*ji* had an inkling that the partition would inevitably lead to riots, and Benaras seemed one of the safest places.'

'Oh, he guessed right.'

'Yes, the riots after Independence were horrendous. Would you believe Pandit*ji* would jump into the crowds to prevent people from fighting? He'd separate people physically and try to calm them down with speeches.'

At first, her obsession with Nehru had worried me, but I soon realised that it was just a habit she had not outgrown. Maybe Nehru was her version of a boy band to obsess over. I knew for a fact that my mother got a little starry eyed whenever she listened to a Bryan Adams song.

'Of course, naani...' I muttered sceptically. Her story did not sound believable in the least.

'He actually did!' she cried defensively.

There was no point arguing with her about someone she worshipped. The last time I tried expressing the idea that Nehru was not as fantastic as she thought, I was compelled to physically remove myself from the room before my grandma turned aggressive.

'So naani, wouldn't you like to meet David again?' I asked abruptly.

She smiled, bemused. She *knew* very well that this was my tactic to avoid discussing her favourite topic.

'Yes...I would, but it is not possible.'

I opened my mouth to say that in this day and age, anything was possible. Technology has made our lives simpler. I had one more week in hand. Considering how terribly selfish I had been before, and how patient my grandma had been, I could at least try to find David.

It would be a lot of work, and I wasn't even sure if the man was alive or not, but I had always liked challenge. And this...well this was an epic challenge that I was determined to overcome.

~

'Hello? Is this Emily Wilson?'

'Yes, who is this?' Emily asked suspiciously. The boy on the other end had an accent she couldn't quite distinguish.

'My name is Aryan Bedi. I am Nandini Sharma's grandson.'

There was a long pause.

Aryan wondered whether she had hung up. He frowned, checking the number he had dialled. He was sure he had made no mistake.

'Oh...hello...' Emily replied, breaking the silence. She didn't really know how to receive a phone call from the grandson of the friend her granddad had betrayed. Should she apologise on behalf of her granddad? Emily wondered.

It had been a week since she had stormed out of her granddad's room. She still wasn't ready to forgive him.

'Um...I know this may sound a bit rude but...your grandfather *is* alive, isn't he?'

Emily nodded, then realised she was on the phone, and smacked herself on the head for her stupidity.

'Erm...yes...I have a slightly rude question as well. How did you find my number?'

'Extensive research on the Internet and a phone directory,' Aryan answered.

He had spent the better part of the past three days frantically browsing the Internet for the slightest trace of David Wilson. He had casually asked his grandma if she had a picture of David, and surprisingly she did have one. What was more surprising to Aryan was that Nandini had given it to him without any questions. Afterwards, Aryan's rigorous efforts to scan and search the image had landed him on a certain Emily Wilson's Facebook page. It was on Emily's photo wall that he had seen one of David's childhood pictures and recognised him immediately.

'That's creepy...' Emily said nervously, coiling the telephone wire around her finger.

'Yeah, well...Don't worry. I'm not some scary forty-year-old pretending to be fifteen. I know that's not entirely convincing but I promise you that I will leave you alone if you just hear me out.' He could hear Emily chuckle nervously at the other end. He knew she was a little wary of him, as she should be.

'I know this is really strange but I... I needed to talk to you. I have a favour to ask of you.'

'Erm...' Aryan cut in before she could get really freaked out and hang up on him.

'Look I know you must be scared, but believe me, my intentions aren't bad. Your grandfather and my grandma were best friends. Your grandfather lived in Lodhi Colony and my grandma's neighbour was his ayah. They became friends because...'

'It's...it's okay. I believe you.' Emily interrupted Aryan. She didn't want to be reminded of the story, which ended with her granddad being the villain.

'All right, great! So if it isn't too much to ask...That is to say, if your grandfather is fit enough to travel, do you think you guys could come to Ranchi by the 13th of August? My... my naani would love to see your grandfather again.'

'But...why?' Emily asked, confused. Hadn't her granddad ruined their friendship? Why would Nandini want to meet a traitor?

'Because they were best friends,' Aryan asserted.

'I know that, but didn't my granddad break his promise to your grandmother?' Emily snapped.

'Yes, but apparently he had fixed everything before leaving.'

'And how did he do that?'

'By releasing my great-grandfather from jail. He would have rotted there for a month or more, if it weren't for your grandfather.'

'Really?' Emily asked, now feeling unbearably guilty about stomping out on her granddad. She had accused him, had felt *disgusted* with him.

Emily felt miserable. She had not even given her granddad a chance to explain. She had just let her words fly recklessly out of her mouth and stalked away like a spoilt brat.

'Yes, really,' Aryan said, rolling his eyes. *Why was she asking stupid questions and wasting his time and money?* Aryan was getting restless. It was expensive to call London from Ranchi, and he was using his pocket money! He'd had to use a payphone so his grandma wouldn't get suspicious.

'Now, if you could come to Ranchi by the 13th, it would be fantastic. Please email me and we can discuss the details. I think this could be great for both our grandparents,'

Emily didn't have much time to think. She wasn't sure if her granddad would *want* to travel with her after how horribly she had treated him. He did deserve to see his friend, and even if it took several sugar free brownies, Emily was determined to get him to go with her.

'Of course, I understand all of that. But why before the 13th?'

'I'll explain it to you when you come. Thank you so much for agreeing to this. Email me soon. Bye.'

Aryan's face split into a huge, satisfied smile. He really was a miracle worker, and an excellent grandson.

Epilogue

'Naani...' Aryan Bedi sang to his grandma, holding her hands and doing a little dance. He looked nothing short of a clown, but today, he was too happy to care.

Away from Aryan and Nandini, Emily Wilson held onto her granddad's hand, feeling rather nervous. She didn't quite know why. She wasn't the one meeting her friend after years of estrangement.

Emily had apologised to David, fumbling with the words that had been spurted out so easily when she was angry with him. He had enveloped her in a warm hug and things had returned back to normal.

'What are you doing, Aryan?' Nandini asked, a little concerned about her grandson's mental well-being. She wondered why Aryan looked unusually happy today. She felt a pang of sadness as she realised it was his last day. Perhaps he was excited about leaving. She thought he had started enjoying his time with her. Maybe she had been wrong...

'I have a surprise for you!' Aryan announced, breaking into her reverie.

'*Arrey*! Where are you going?' she called after him, completely bewildered. She had no idea what was going on.

'To get your surprise,' he walked up to where Emily was hiding, and smiled brightly at the granddaughter and the grandfather.

'Hi, I'm Aryan, very nice to meet you,' he extended his hand and Emily shook it nervously. David grinned at Aryan.

'All right, are you two ready?'

The pair nodded, and Aryan led them to the garden, where Nandini was sitting.

'Naani, this is your surprise…' he stepped aside, and Nandini frowned as she saw a British man, who looked her age, clutching his granddaughter's hand.

'Who is this?' Nandini asked, eyeing them, confused. She had half a mind to call security, and then drive Aryan to the hospital. Maybe he had taken a few sneaky sips of the wine his mother had sent for her.

'Naani, meet Emily and David Wilson,' Aryan announced proudly, as his grandma's expression changed from confusion to utter shock. He hoped dearly that she was pleasantly surprised. With wobbly knees, she got up from her seat. Aryan ran to support her as she took shaky steps, but David beat him to it. For an eighty-three-year-old man, he was incredibly fit.

'David Wilson…' Nandini breathed, staring at him in disbelief.

'Nandini Sharma,' David replied, his eyes twinkling, with mischief…*or was it happiness?*

Neither Emily nor Aryan could comprehend it. They were spectators, silently watching the reunion of two friends. They had done their part by bringing the two together.

Nandini removed her hand from David's grip, slowly raising it to his face. Trembling, she touched his face with her fingertips, and her eyes widened. She spread her fingers across his right cheek, her face breaking into a smile.

Aryan and Emily watched the exchange with smiles identical to their grandparents'.

'So why were you so insistent on us being here on the 13th?' Emily asked Aryan, turning away from her grandparents.

She figured it would be better to give the pair some privacy. After all, they had years to catch up on, and probably would not like their grandchildren staring at them as if they were museum exhibits.

'You'll see. Wait for two minutes,' Aryan said, taking Emily's cue and turning away from Nandini and David as well. Before Emily could ask anything else, he walked away from her, disappearing into the house. When he returned, he had a silver tray in his hand. Emily squinted against the bright sun, trying to make sense of the objects arranged on the plate. Beaming from ear to ear, Aryan moved toward Nandini and David, hiding the tray behind.

'Uh...excuse me?'

The reunited friends turned to look at him, smiling.

'Sorry to interrupt you, but I have another surprise for you,' Aryan grinned again, swaying from side-to-side, his hands behind his back.

'He's a lot like you,' David remarked and Aryan blushed. His grandma smirked at him, immediately receiving a scowl that reminded David so much of a young Nandini.

'Happy birthday, naani,' Aryan slowly revealed the hidden tray and put a *teeka* on her forehead. His grandma wore an expression that he couldn't quite decipher. There was a sort of overwhelming warmth that filled her eyes. She was smiling, so he guessed that it wasn't sadness. He had forgotten the *diya*, but it didn't matter to Nandini. She was unbelievably touched that he had remembered the tradition. Frankly she was surprised to know that he listened to her story at all.

What astounded her ever more, however, was when Aryan bent down and touched her feet. She blessed him, teary-eyed. When he straightened up, she pulled his cheek, and planted a kiss on his forehead. He made a face and stepped aside.

'Naani...' he whined, and David laughed at the duo's emotional exchange. Aryan was *exactly* like the young Nandini he had known. Nandini scowled at David, knowing *exactly* what was going on in his mind.

'I'm guessing you were too lazy to get me a gift,' Nandini said teasingly, the sunlight dancing in her eyes, the corners creased.

'Well, look at the pot calling the kettle black!' exclaimed David, earning a glare from Nandini like old times. David removed the bag slung across his shoulders, unzipped the top and retrieved something wrapped in bright-green paper. Straining to keep a straight face, he handed it to Nandini. Nandini could see the orange peeking from beneath the folds.

'Chandni Chowk's jalebis!' Nandini exclaimed, as she discovered the contents inside.

'Your favourite.'

David chuckled at the sight of his friend attacking the jalebis with a ferocity that was almost desperation. He saw the fourteen-year-old Nandini standing right in front of him—who devoured the jalebis within minutes—whom he had left behind eons ago.

Not much had changed. Only a few inches, strands of grey hair and failing knees were introduced into their life in the time that they had been apart.

'Excuse me sir! Can I ask you something?' Aryan interrupted David's stream of thought.

'Yes, of course, and please, call me David.'

Aryan nodded and shuffled awkwardly keeping his gaze lowered. David couldn't get over how similar he was to his friend.

'Well I...I wanted to know how my naani...came to know...' Aryan mumbled, chewing at his bottom lip. With a shoe dug into the soft, wet mud, he waited expectantly for an answer.

'Came to know what?' David asked.

Aryan took a deep breath and motivated himself to speak again.

'How did she come to know that you bailed her father?'

There was a silence—tense and stretched—like a rubber band being dragged down by weights for a physics experiment. It snapped when Aryan's shoe squeaked in the mud.

'I have absolutely no idea what you are talking about,' David replied, and without waiting for the imminent reaction, from Aryan, began walking in the direction of the house. Aryan stood still for a minute, feeling frustrated yet again. What was it with these two being so smug and mysterious about their story? With the tantalisingly delicious smell of jalebis wafting his way, he was forced to join in the celebration. Food took precedence over anything. The answer could wait. He could afford more sleepless nights, trying to deconstruct both his grandma's and David's cryptic replies.

As he took a bite of the jalebi his grandma handed him so reluctantly, he realised it wouldn't be the end of the world if he didn't find out. It was David and Nandini's story. Whether they wanted to tell all of it, or keep some of it to themselves was entirely their decision.

~

Acknowledgements

A big 'Thank you' to my family for their undying support; my friends and professors who helped me with the research and everyone else who contributed in their own way.

Fragments of Pandit Jawaharlal Nehru's speeches have been sourced from *Important Speeches of Jawaharlal Nehru*, edited by Jagat S. Bright.